"There is one front and one battle where everyone in the United States—every man, woman, and child—is in action, and will be privileged to remain in action throughout this war. That front is right here at home, in our daily lives, and in our daily tasks."

—President Franklin D. Roosevelt, April 28, 1942

Under the Apple Tree

WHISTLE STOP
Café
≡ MYSTERIES ≡

# UNDER the APPLE TREE

## GABRIELLE MEYER

Guideposts

# UNDER the APPLE TREE

# CHAPTER ONE

Dust motes floated on the warm, thick air as Debbie Albright shoved a cardboard box into the corner of her attic. A sneeze started to build in her nose, forcing her to stop what she was doing and hold her hand above her lip. Her eyes watered, but the feeling soon passed.

"Your allergies will never survive this move." Janet Shaw, Debbie's best friend, tossed her a box of tissues. "Should we take a break? The coffee shop has half-priced mochas on Saturdays."

Debbie pulled a tissue free. "We don't have time for a break. I want to get all the storage boxes out of the living room before Ian gets here with the furniture." He would be arriving any minute, and Debbie and Janet still had several more trips to make up the two flights of stairs to the attic.

The air was hot and stuffy, and a hundred years' worth of dust lined the cracks and crevices of the old shiplap on the ceiling and walls. Beneath her feet, the boards creaked in protest, reminding Debbie that the home was old and she had a big job ahead of her. But she couldn't be happier or more excited to finally be back in Dennison, Ohio. The beautiful craftsman-style bungalow she had purchased would need quite a bit of work, but she wasn't afraid to tackle the project, especially with her friends' help.

"It looks like Mr. Zink left a few treasures for you," Janet commented. The lid on an old trunk creaked in protest as she lifted it.

"He mentioned that his nieces and nephews left a few odds and ends." Debbie shoved the used tissue into the pocket of her overalls as she moved around several boxes to join Janet. "But he said most of it would probably need to be thrown away."

"This looks like it's full of old newspapers." Janet bent down and lifted one from the trunk, her blue eyes opening wide. "This is from December, 1941."

Debbie took the paper from Janet and slipped one of her brown curls back into the bandanna tied around her head. Despite the heat, a chill climbed up her spine as she read the headline. "'War Declared.'" Even though it had happened before her lifetime, she still felt a keen tug in her heart when she thought about World War II. "I can't even imagine what it would have been like to live through such a difficult time."

Janet lifted more newspapers out of the trunk. "Some of these are from the *Dennison Daily Transcript* and talk about all the troops coming through the depot."

"I could read these for hours."

Janet stood up straight. "We'll have to go through all this later."

"I probably won't have much free time, even after I'm settled." Not with all the work she had to do on the house and the plans they had to open the Whistle Stop Café in the old train depot a few blocks up the street. After leaving her corporate job in Cleveland, Debbie had come back to town to do just that. Somehow, she'd convinced Janet to help her, knowing what an amazing cook and baker her best friend had become over the years. Janet had worked for the Third

Street Bakery for much of her career and was ready to start her own business. Their grand opening would be in three weeks, which meant they still had a massive amount of work ahead of them.

As Debbie lowered the newspaper back into the trunk, something else caught her attention. "What's this?"

An olive-green metal box with the stenciled words SPECIAL SERVICES, US ARMY sat at the bottom of the trunk. Leather straps on the sides made it easy for Debbie to lift out, but they were stiff and cracked with age. She was afraid they would break.

Janet watched as Debbie set the metal box on the dusty floor.

"It's definitely military issue, whatever it is." Debbie ran her fingers along the stenciled words. Iron corner protectors and rivets lined the seams, while clasps held the top and bottom together. "And it's old," she added.

"I bet it's from the 1940s, like the newspapers." Janet squatted next to Debbie. "Do you think it belonged to Mr. Zink?"

"I'm sure it did. He was an infantryman during the war. He fought in Europe and came home to tell about it."

"Do you think he meant to leave it when he moved?" Janet leaned over to inspect the side of the box.

"I don't know." Debbie unhooked the clasps and gently pulled upward. The hinges groaned, but the box held a wonderful surprise. "It's a portable phonograph!"

"I didn't even know there was such a thing way back then."

The phonograph was in great shape for its age. "Who would ever guess that such an ugly box could house such a beautiful instrument?"

"Do you know how it works?"

Debbie had seen one similar to it in an antique store once, and the owner had shown her how it worked, but the one she'd seen had been in a lot worse shape. "If I remember correctly..." She lifted a handle from the bottom left-hand corner and inserted it into the front of the box. It was curved, and she used it to crank the mechanism. When it was tight, she reached up and shifted a lever, and the turntable began to spin.

"Amazing!" Janet's voice held awe. "I can't believe it still works."

"These things are worth a lot of money," Debbie said. "I need to let Mr. Zink know he forgot to take it."

"Do you think maybe..." Janet rose and went back to the trunk where she moved the rest of the newspapers. "Bingo!" She lifted a thin cardboard sheath.

Debbie smiled as she took the small record. The label in the center had a handwritten note on it, which she read out loud. "'To Ray, with love, Eleanor.'" Under that was the song title, "Don't Sit Under the Apple Tree (With Anyone Else but Me)."

Janet stared at the record. "Do you think Ray is Mr. Zink?"

Debbie nodded. "His first name is Raymond." She flipped off the turntable and let it come to a stop and then set the record on it before pushing the lever again. Her heart pounded as she lifted the needle and gently set it on the record, hoping she knew what she was doing. The last thing she wanted to do was damage the record or the phonograph.

The noise was scratchy at first, and then a clear, beautiful voice filled the attic, singing a version of the Andrews Sisters' popular song.

Debbie looked up and met Janet's surprised gaze. "Who do you think Eleanor was?"

"Whoever she was, she had a great voice."

"This sounds like an amateur recording," Debbie said. "I wonder if she was Mr. Zink's sweetheart."

"He never got married, did he?" Janet asked. "I wonder what happened to Eleanor."

Debbie perked up when she heard a noise from downstairs. "It sounds like Ian is here."

Janet sighed. "I was hoping we could listen to the other records in the trunk." She shrugged. "There'll be time later, I suppose."

Debbie lifted the needle and switched off the turntable. As Janet rose and went to the stairs to greet her husband, Debbie gently slid the record back into its sheath.

Mr. Zink must have forgotten that the phonograph and records were in the attic. It didn't seem right to keep them from him. As soon as she had a bit of free time, she'd stop by the assisted-living home and ask him what he wanted her to do with the trunk.

It would give her a chance to visit with the elderly man again and give him an update on her big move. He'd always been one of her favorite people, full of fun stories and interesting historical tidbits about Dennison. She would take any excuse she could find to stop in and visit.

The portable phonograph, not to mention Eleanor's record, was the perfect reason.

The next day, Debbie had a few minutes after church to stop in and visit Raymond Zink. He had moved into the Good Shepherd

Retirement Center a couple of months earlier, after deciding to sell his home to Debbie. She was familiar with the Good Shepherd, since her dad had recently retired from managing the facility.

Debbie passed through the front doors and into the cozy foyer. The sitting room was full of residents and their families, and she smiled at several people she knew. Though she hadn't lived in Dennison for almost twenty years, she had come home often and stayed in touch with many of her childhood friends and their family members. It was comforting to return to her old church, see her former schoolteachers downtown, run into an old neighbor at the grocery store, and generally feel at home again. Cleveland had never felt so tight-knit or full of a sense of community. At least, not in the same way as her hometown.

Debbie stopped at the front desk with the record and phonograph. A volunteer sat there with a smile on his face.

"Good afternoon," he said. "I'm Steven. How can I help you?"

"Hi, Steven." Debbie returned his smile. "I'm looking for Raymond Zink."

"Ray?" Steven's grin widened. "He's holding court in the dining room this afternoon."

"Holding court?"

Steven shook his head as he chuckled. "You'll see. Dining room is that way and to the left." He pointed in the direction she should go.

"Thank you. Mind if I leave this phonograph here? It belongs to Mr. Zink, but it's a little heavy to haul around."

"Sure. I'll have someone take it to Ray's room for you, if you'd like."

"That would be great." She smiled as she walked down the hall, following the smell of pot roast and baked bread.

Even before she turned the corner into the dining room, she could hear Mr. Zink's voice. It was loud and clear, and he was telling the story of Old Bing, the service dog that had gone to war with the Gray brothers of Dennison in June of 1918.

Debbie stopped inside the doorway and listened as Mr. Zink continued his story. He sat in his wheelchair, near the upright piano, one of his hands resting on the ivory keys, as if he'd just finished playing a song. He was famous in Dennison for his piano playing.

Sitting around him were about a dozen people. Some looked like they were residents, while others appeared to be visiting family members. Mr. Zink held everyone's attention, from the youngest to the oldest.

"Bing was only nine days old when he was smuggled onto a troop ship by the Gray brothers, one hundred and five years ago this month," Mr. Zink said. "He went through basic training and served in active duty, with fifty-eight days in the trenches, and received two citations for bravery." Mr. Zink's body showed his advanced age, but his eyes lit up and his voice was strong as he spoke. "Old Bing survived being gassed twice and came back to Dennison with yellow teeth and patches of missing fur from the side effects. But for his service in the First World War, he received the regular sixty-eight-dollar bonus for discharged soldiers."

Debbie had heard the story of Old Bing before, but she never tired of it. When Mr. Zink saw her standing there, his face brightened with a smile and he excused himself from his audience to join her, pushing the wheels on his chair.

"Hello, Debbie. It's so nice to see you again."

"Hello, Mr. Zink." Debbie knew him from growing up in her church. When she decided to come back to Dennison to open the Whistle Stop Café, he heard she was looking for a house and offered his. It was almost miraculous how everything had fallen into place. "I'm happy to see you've found a new audience to share your passion for history."

"I won't stop until the Good Lord takes me home." He motioned to a chair. "First of all, everyone here calls me Ray. Second, have a seat and tell me why you're here. I hope everything is okay at the house."

"It's perfect. I love it." She set her bag down and pulled out the old record inside its sheath. "I actually came by to let you know there was a trunk left in the attic and I thought you might want it."

"A trunk?" Ray squinted. "What was in it?"

"Some newspapers, a portable phonograph, which is being delivered to your room, and this." She handed him the record.

Ray looked at it for a moment and then slowly slipped the record out of the sheath. His mouth began to quiver, and his gaze seemed to slip back in time. "My Eleanor." Finally, he looked at Debbie. "Where did you say you found this?"

"In an old trunk in the attic," she repeated, watching him closely. "I thought maybe you had forgotten it."

"I hadn't forgotten—how could I forget about her?" He held the record to his chest. "I haven't been able to get into that attic for almost a decade, and I was sure I'd lost this. I can't believe you found it."

"Who was she?" Debbie asked. "She had a beautiful singing voice."

"It was only a small part of her beauty." Tears filled Ray's eyes as he spoke. "I've never known a woman like Eleanor O'Reilly before or since."

"Was she your sweetheart?"

"She was more than that. She was my very heart and soul." He looked at the record again and tenderly ran his hand over the label. "She was supposed to be my wife."

"What happened to her?" Debbie asked.

He shook his head. "I don't know."

Debbie frowned. "You don't know?"

"When I left Dennison to join the army, she was standing on the platform at the depot to see me off. She promised to write and told me that when I returned, we'd be married." He swallowed and let out a sad sigh. "But her letters stopped abruptly, and when I came home, she wasn't here. I looked for her for months, but I never saw her again. I eventually came to the realization that she didn't love me. It was the only explanation I could come to." He was quiet for a moment, lost in his own thoughts. "I never loved again."

Debbie's heart broke for Ray. She had lost her fiancé when he died in Afghanistan as a special forces officer. It had been years, but sometimes it felt like yesterday. Would the pain remain with her as long as it had with Ray? The thought felt weighty and suffocating.

"Debbie?" Ray asked.

"Yes?"

"Would you help me find Eleanor? She probably doesn't want to hear from me, if she's still alive, but I've always wondered where she went and how she made out. It would do my heart good to know she was happy."

Debbie smiled. Though she had a house to remodel and a restaurant to open in less than three weeks, how could she say no to such a heartfelt request? "I'd love to help you."

His lips trembled, but his smile was radiant. "Can I tell you how I met Eleanor?" he asked.

Debbie couldn't wait to find out.

# CHAPTER TWO

*June 11, 1943*

*Raymond Zink had never encountered a morning he
didn't like, and today was no different. He whistled as
he stacked a pile of crates in the kitchen at the Dennison
Depot Canteen. He didn't know what was inside them,
but they'd just come in on the back of a farmer's truck
from the Sugarcreek area. He'd been told to bring them
here, where a handful of ladies chatted and scurried
about as they busily constructed hundreds of sandwiches for the next troop train that would soon arrive.*

*Stopping for a minute to wipe his brow with his
handkerchief, he shook his head in wonder at the ladies
assembled. There were girls as young as eight or nine,
running for supplies and doing their mamas' bidding,
and women as old as eighty-five or ninety, cutting open
buns, slicing meat, packaging sandwiches, and filling
little paper bags with cookies, candy, or doughnuts.*

Women and a few men of every age in between ensured that food would be ready for the troops.

And Ray was there, doing his part as well—though he'd rather be fighting. He'd been hired by the railroad to be a man-of-all-work a year and a half ago, when the war broke out. But now, less than two weeks shy of his eighteenth birthday, all he could think about was volunteering to go overseas. Each train that went through Dennison was another reminder that he was getting close, and soon, he'd be on his way too.

But not today. Today, he was in his hometown, serving the troops who were going to fight when he couldn't— and he was doing it with a smile.

"Hello, Raymond," Mabel Thomas said as she stood on the end of the assembly line, putting the sandwiches into wax-paper bags. "Will you be at the canteen dance tonight?"

He paused and leaned on the dolly cart. Mabel knew full well that he was going to be at the dance. Ray played the piano every Friday night for the canteen dances. They were held to raise money for the food and supplies needed to feed the men.

"You know I'll be there, Mabel." He winked at her, knowing she wanted him to ask her if she'd like an escort. "Will you?"

Mabel was seventeen, the same age as Ray. They'd known each other since the first day of school, and she'd been mooning after him ever since. He didn't mind. Mabel was pretty and sweet, but he thought of her more like a sister than anything else.

"I'll be there," she said, her cheeks turning pink. "I'll be wearing that yellow dress you like so well."

"Keep moving." One of the matronly ladies elbowed the poor girl in the ribs.

Mabel jumped and turned to the woman, a frown on her freckled forehead. Embarrassment tinged the tip of her nose, and Ray thought to spare her from more humiliation, so he started whistling again and pushed the dolly toward the door.

It was warm inside the depot where the Salvation Army's railroad canteen had been set up, but no one seemed to notice. All they were focused on was making enough sandwiches, filling enough coffeepots, and preparing enough magazines, religious literature, and little trinkets to hand out to the servicemen and women who would come through. Since April of last year they'd been working almost around the clock to meet each troop train. They weren't slowing down either. Each month, they seemed to be serving more and more soldiers. The volunteers kept pouring in too, from all parts *of Ohio. Mothers, daughters, wives, sweethearts, sisters, and friends all wanted to do their part.*

*Ray had never been in a beehive, but he imagined the railroad canteen was as close as he'd ever get. Everyone was busy, moving this way and that, bumping into each other, always pushing or pulling or moving something. A constant buzz was in the air as the ladies visited, gossiped, and shared news about their men. Day and night, from five in the morning to midnight, the canteen hummed with activity. Since the troop trains' movements were classified, no one knew for certain when the next one would come through. Sometimes they had hours between trains—and other times just minutes.*

*When Ray was almost to the door, he paused— stopped dead in his tracks—and nearly tripped over the dolly he maneuvered through the crowded space.*

*Eileen Turner, the new stationmaster, stood near the door with a young woman Ray had never laid eyes on before in his life. The woman—or really girl, since she couldn't have been more than seventeen or eighteen, had flaxen-blond hair, curled at the edges, and a blue ribbon tied around her head that perfectly matched her eyes. He'd seen lots of pretty girls before, but this one was different. She was more than pretty— she was lovely.*

For the first time in his life, Ray understood what it felt like to be dumbstruck. He could do nothing but stand there and gawk at the new girl, wondering where she had come from and how long she would be staying.

A few of the older ladies started to whisper and chuckle, and he realized they were talking about him.

"Need some help, Ray?" one of them asked. "We've never seen you looking so helpless before."

Another round of chuckles followed that statement as Eileen moved into the depot with the girl and introduced her to some of the Salvation Army workers. She was probably a new volunteer, but would she be there for the day? The week? Indefinitely? Most of the surrounding communities volunteered one day a week. Today was Sugarcreek's day, with Dennison citizens filling in wherever and whenever needed. But there were a few ladies who came to stay with friends and family in Dennison and worked at the canteen every chance they could get. What kind of volunteer was she?

He had to find out.

A truck horn honked outside, and Ray remembered the task he'd been given.

"Ray," said another lady, "you're slacking. That farmer doesn't want to wait all day."

Eileen and the new girl looked in his direction, but Ray wasn't about to embarrass himself further. If he *didn't get out to the waiting farmer, the man would come looking for him and cause a scene. So Ray left the depot to get the rest of the crates from the truck.*

*"Thought you forgot about me," the farmer said with a scowl. "I don't got all day, you know."*

*"Yes, sir," Ray said as he started to stack the remaining crates on his dolly. He could easily manage five, but there were seven left.*

*"You'll need to come back for the rest," the farmer said to him. "Be quick about it."*

*"I can handle a couple more crates," Ray said, standing up taller to puff out his chest. Maybe he'd impress the new girl if she saw him toting so many heavy boxes.*

*"I can wait," the farmer said. "But not long."*

*"I'll take them now." Ray stacked another crate on the first five. This one came up to the top of the dolly handle.*

*"Don't be a fool," the farmer said.*

*"I can manage. I do it every day." Ray took the last crate and put it on the top. It wobbled a bit, but he was strong and capable. He knew his way around the canteen with a dolly.*

*"Suit yourself." The farmer closed the back of the truck, walked around, and jumped inside the cab.*

"Thank you," Ray managed to say before the farmer pulled away from the station, his wheels kicking up gravel as he left.

For a minute, Ray stared at the crates, rethinking his plan. He'd have to rest the top crate against his chest to keep it from falling, but it wouldn't be all bad. He could show off his muscles in the process.

Carefully, he balanced the load as he started back toward the depot. The sun was hot and the air was humid, causing sweat to break out on his forehead. Slowly, he made his way to the door and was just about to turn inside when Eileen and the new girl appeared on the threshold.

"Whoa!" Ray said as he lost control of the stack of crates, trying not to run into the ladies. The top crate came crashing to the floor, within feet of the new girl. When the lid popped off, several gallon jars of pickles came crashing out and splashed pickle juice all over her legs and skirt.

She paused, stunned, and looked down at her sopping dress.

Ray had to do some fancy footwork to keep the other crates from falling.

"Ray!" Eileen said in shock and surprise. "What are you doing?"

*The new girl finally looked up at him, her eyes wide as she blinked.*

*He felt tongue-tied again, completely captivated by those eyes—but now she was covered in pickle juice, and it was all his fault.*

*"I'm sorry," Ray said as he bent down to pick up the pieces of glass. Thankfully, he'd only broken three of the jars, but they were big and had caused a mess. Pickles and juice circled the new girl's feet, so that no matter which way she walked, she'd be stepping on the tart little cucumbers. "I hope your heels aren't ruined."*

*"Ray," Eileen said, "this is Eleanor O'Reilly. Eleanor, this is Raymond Zink, the man-of-all-work at the station. He's usually not this clumsy."*

*Ray stood and wanted to extend his hand to shake Eleanor's, but it was full of glass. "How do you do, Miss O'Reilly," he said, his voice sounding kind of wobbly. He knew he looked like an idiot, and his feelings were probably written all over his face. It was one of his worst qualities—he could never hide his true feelings.*

*"How do you do," Eleanor said, lowering her eyes and causing her long, dark lashes to brush against her high cheekbones.*

*Ray was smitten. As good as gone. He felt his knees going weak just looking at her. What kind of a fool was he? No one had ever made him react this way. He* was smart enough to know that looks weren't every-thing. But there was something about this girl that told him her beauty wasn't only skin-deep.

Eileen lifted an eyebrow at him and shook her head. At twenty, she was young to be a stationmaster, but the last one had been called to active duty, and Eileen was there to fill the position. Though she was brand-new at her job, she was in full command, and she would have a word with Ray later, he was certain. "Eleanor is a new volunteer who just came to town. She'll be boarding with the Snodgrass family for now."

So she was staying in town—and at the Snodgrass house! That was directly across the street from where Ray lived with his parents and little sister, Gayle.

"Why don't I take you to the Snodgrasses' so you can clean up before you get to work," Eileen said to Eleanor.

"Yes, ma'am—miss—" Eleanor seemed at a loss for words herself. "I would appreciate that."

Eileen smiled. "Call me Eileen," she said, "same as everyone else. We don't have time to be formal around here."

"I'd be happy to escort Miss O'Reilly home," Ray said quickly. "It's the least I can do, since the pickles are my fault."

Eileen had known Ray his whole life and knew that he lived across from the Snodgrass family. She nodded.

*"All right, but hurry back. We need all the help we can get. I'll have someone else clean up this mess."*

*Ray dropped the glass into a nearby garbage can and then motioned for Eleanor to follow him.*

*As they started the walk toward the Snodgrass house, he wished he didn't stink like garlic and dill pickles. But he took consolation in knowing that Eleanor did as well.*

*Ray dropped Eleanor off and ran across the street to change his pants in the bungalow his dad had built in 1924, when he and Ray's mother were first married. His mom called out to him to grab the picnic basket by the front door, which she had filled with buns to donate to the canteen, and Gayle begged to come with him, since she was out of school for the summer and looking for something to do. But he barely acknowledged either one of them as he grabbed the buns and raced back to the Snodgrass house.*

*There, he paced outside for what seemed like an eternity—when it was probably more like fifteen minutes.*

*Mrs. Snodgrass, who was one of Mama's best friends, came outside to see what all the fuss was about.*

When she realized it was just Ray and he was waiting for Eleanor, she smiled in that way older women do, as if she knew something he didn't, and went back inside.

Ray had never felt so nervous or excited in his life. Since the moment he'd laid eyes on Eleanor, his insides had felt all jumbled. How was it possible that he felt like he'd known her his whole life when they'd only exchanged a handful of words?

What if she didn't feel the same way? He had made such a fool of himself. What if she didn't give him the time of day?

He stopped pacing and tried not to worry—which was already a lost cause. He'd never felt like this before and doubted he'd ever feel this way again.

Finally, the front door opened, and Eleanor stepped out in a fresh dress, this one pink, with a matching ribbon in her hair.

How was it possible that she looked even prettier than before?

She lowered her gaze when she caught him staring, and her cheeks filled with color.

"You look pretty," he said.

"Thank you."

They started to walk back toward the depot. It was only four blocks away, so he knew he had to make the time count.

WHISTLE STOP CAFÉ MYSTERIES

"Eileen said you just came into town," he said. "Where'd you come from?"

"New Philadelphia, by the Tuscarawas River. I wanted to be here in Dennison so I could volunteer as much as possible."

Her voice was so lyrical, he had to concentrate on her words.

New Philadelphia was about ten miles away. Close enough that he was familiar with the town but far enough away that he'd never met or heard of Eleanor O'Reilly— much to his chagrin. "Are you going to miss your folks?"

"I don't have any." Her voice was sad, and he immediately felt bad for asking.

"I'm sorry—"

"Don't be. You didn't know. I was raised by the Murdocks. They're a couple from my church who took me in after my parents died in an automobile accident when I was ten. As soon as I turned eighteen, just yesterday, I left and don't plan to ever go back. I couldn't wait for my birthday. My parents left me some money I can live on until I find permanent work."

"I'll be eighteen in two weeks," Ray said. "I can't wait for my birthday either."

Her eyes lit up. "Are you wanting to go somewhere too?"

Ray lifted his chin, his chest extending. "I'm going to enlist in the army."

Eleanor frowned and looked down at the road as they walked.

"Why?" he asked. "Where do you want to go?"

"New York City." She didn't hesitate, and the sparkle returned to her eyes. "I'm going to be a singer."

Ray paused and drew her to a stop on the sidewalk. "You sing?"

Her cheeks colored again. "I love singing. I had so many chores at the Murdocks' that I had to do something to keep my spirits up, so I sang and sang and sang." She lifted her shoulders and looked to the sky. "And now I want to sing to celebrate my freedom."

"Will you sing for me?" he asked, still not ready to reach the canteen.

"Here?" She laughed and shook her head. "Right on the street?"

"Sure, why not?" He looked around. "There's no one out here."

Eleanor bit her bottom lip, her eyes dancing with glee. "Okay. What would you like me to sing?"

"What's your favorite?"

"I love the Andrews Sisters."

"Then sing something from them."

*Eleanor looked right and left, as if she was afraid someone was hiding behind a tree. Finally, she said, "Do you know 'Don't Sit Under the Apple Tree'?"*

*Ray grinned from ear to ear and nodded. He loved that song.*

*Lifting her chin, Eleanor began to sing.*

*Her voice was amazing. Prettier, even, than any of the Andrews Sisters. She bounced as she sang, her head tipping back and forth, and her voice filled the neighborhood. So much joy bubbled out of her, she seemed hardly able to contain herself. And that joy filled Ray too. He'd never felt anything like it. He could have listened to her all day.*

*If he thought he was a goner before, now he was certain. Eleanor was meant for singing—or singing was meant for her.*

*And he and she were meant for each other. He just knew it.*

*When she finished, he was still grinning. "Would you sing for the canteen dance? I play piano every Friday night—it's a fundraiser, and all the neighboring towns come in to dance. Sometimes a train will come in with troops, and some of them like to dance for a few minutes too. It's a lot of fun. We've never had a* singer before. It's always only been me on the piano. Would you sing tonight?"

Eleanor swallowed hard. "In front of a crowd?"

"I know they'd love it," he said. "Please—I'd like it too. If you want to sing in New York City, you'll need to start somewhere, right? Why not start in Dennison, Ohio? It's called Dreamsville, USA, for a reason, you know."

"Is it? Why is it called Dreamsville?"

"The soldiers started calling it that because of the canteen and the Glenn Miller song, 'Dreamsville, Ohio.' Dennison is a pretty sweet place, just like the town in the song." He knew she was stalling, so he said, "Will you sing for us tonight, Eleanor?"

She pressed her lips together, as if she was thinking hard, and then she nodded. "Okay. I'll sing tonight. If you promise me you'll be there."

"Of course I'll be there—playing piano the whole time. Even if I wasn't, I'd still be there." He wanted to tell her again that she was pretty, or try to explain this strange feeling he had about her—like she was going to be the most important person in his life.

He wanted to tell her that from the moment he saw her, he knew he was going to marry her. But he couldn't—and he wouldn't. He'd scare her off for sure.

They kept walking, and his hand brushed against hers, but she didn't move it away.

"Are you always this sweet, Raymond Zink?" she asked. "To all the girls, I mean?"

For a long time, Ray didn't answer. He couldn't. He was sweet to all the girls—had even flirted with many of them—but he'd never taken his feelings for them seriously.

"I think you are sweet to all of them." Eleanor answered for him, but she didn't sound angry or upset. "It's who God made you to be."

If Ray didn't move fast, he knew Eleanor would get her head turned by one of the other guys. Either a volunteer who came in to help at the canteen, or one of the servicemen who came through on the troop trains. Lots of guys asked the girls for their names and addresses so they could write, and Ray had even heard about one soldier who had proposed to a volunteer— and she had said yes! He couldn't take that chance.

"I might be sweet to the other girls," he finally said. He tentatively took her hand in his, waiting for her to pull away. When she didn't, he felt bolder to say, "But you're the only girl who has ever made me feel this way."

She dipped her head but didn't protest.

He could have jumped to the clouds, he was so happy.

But he only squeezed her hand a little tighter, thanking God that he wasn't eighteen yet and he could spend the next couple of weeks with Eleanor O'Reilly.

# CHAPTER THREE

*D*ebbie rolled down the windows of her car to allow the fresh air to blow through her hair. She had thoroughly enjoyed her afternoon visit with Ray, hearing all about how he had met Eleanor O'Reilly. Their visit was cut short when the staff came in to announce that bingo would begin shortly. Since Ray never missed a bingo game, Debbie had left after promising to return on a different day to bring the trunk full of old newspapers.

But, in the meantime, she was determined to see what she could find out about Eleanor and her disappearance. It seemed so strange that Eleanor and Ray would have had such a quick bond and then she would leave him while he served overseas and never make contact again. Had something nefarious happened?

Debbie turned onto Center Street, where the depot came into view. It took all her willpower not to stop and see if the contractor, Dale, had put in the new counter stools that were delivered the day before. He had said he'd get to it before he and his men left for the evening, but she thought he might have been a little too optimistic about it.

And she had been too busy with unpacking boxes at her house yesterday afternoon to stop in and see for herself.

With a sigh, Debbie turned down North Fifth Street to head home. She was just the third owner since the house was built in

1924, and she took her ownership seriously. She planned to do everything within her power to retain the historical integrity of the home while updating it and bringing it into the twenty-first century. And today she would start.

A red pickup truck was parked on the street in front of Debbie's house with the words CONNOR CONSTRUCTION on the driver's side door.

Greg Connor, the contractor she had hired to work on her house, was early—which was a good sign. After working with Dale at the depot, she had decided to hire someone else for her house projects. Greg specialized in flipping properties, but he was also a renovation consultant and had come highly recommended from a few friends and neighbors. Debbie's dad had offered to help her, and though he was retired and eager to have something to do, she didn't want to ask him to do all the work.

After parking her car in the driveway, Debbie got out and walked toward the street. Greg also got out of his truck—and Debbie was struck by how young he looked. For some reason, she had pictured someone her dad's age, but Greg Connor was at least twenty years younger—closer to her age. He opened the back passenger-side door, and a beautiful black-and-white border collie jumped out and stood by his side.

"Debbie?" Greg asked. He took off his sunglasses, revealing stunning blue eyes. He was a head taller than she, with dark brown hair graying at the temples. He was clean-shaven and wore a pair of blue jeans and a red polo shirt with a Connor Construction logo. When he smiled, a deep dimple appeared in each cheek, making him instantly likable.

"Yes," she said, extending her hand to shake his. "Thank you for coming on a Sunday to check things out. I'm in a little bit of a time crunch."

"I understand." His handshake was strong and firm, his skin rough from work. He held a clipboard under his arm. "Being self-employed pretty much means being available 24-7. I don't mind." He motioned toward the house. "You got yourself a great house. It's a perfect example of the craftsman era, not to mention that it's solidly built."

"You're familiar with the house?"

"Ray is like a grandfather to me. He was my grandfather's friend and took my boys and me under his wing after my wife passed away five years ago. We've had many meals around his kitchen table."

"You're from Dennison, then?"

"Born and raised. I left after high school for a few years to go to college before coming back for good. I have two sons, one in seventh grade and one in ninth. Dennison is home."

His name had sounded familiar though they hadn't gone to high school together. He probably graduated before she started. "I've heard great things about you and your work. I was even told that you're the president of the chamber of commerce."

He looked down at his feet, and his humility was heartwarming. "I do what I can."

"I know you usually flip houses and don't do a lot of remodeling work for homeowners, but I was hoping you might be able to help me."

"I'm happy to take a look. I've done a few other projects on the side. If I can help you, I will." He put his hand on the dog's head.

"This is Hammer. As you said, I'm usually flipping houses, so he goes inside with me, since no one is living in them. I don't know how you feel about dogs. He can wait in the truck for me if you'd rather he not come in."

Debbie smiled. "I think he'll be fine. He seems like a well-behaved pooch." When she held out her hand, Hammer trotted over to her and welcomed the attention with a fiercely wagging tail.

She motioned for Greg to follow her to the house. "Right now, my biggest concern is to get the guest rooms ready for a couple of visitors I have coming in three weeks for the café's grand opening."

"We're all excited about that," he said. "I'm looking forward to seeing what you do with the place. My grandfather left from the depot in May of 1942 to head to Europe, so it's always had a special meaning to me."

She nodded as she unlocked the front door. "It's an important piece of Dennison's past—but also the nation's past. There aren't many railroad canteens left standing." She motioned to the boxes stacked up in her enclosed porch. "Please ignore the mess. I'm still moving in, and I have a lot of work ahead of me."

"I understand." He chuckled. "At least you have an excuse. I live with two teenage boys, and I'm always tripping over something in my house."

Debbie smiled. It was easy to talk to Greg Connor. He was confident but comfortable to be around, putting her at ease.

"Over time," she said as she led him through another door and into the foyer, "I would like to repaint the rooms and have the wood floors refinished. Some of the light fixtures need to be changed, and the kitchen cabinets will have to be replaced. But…" She stopped and pointed at the built-in parson's bench in the foyer. "The woodwork in this place is stunning. I won't have to do a thing to it, except maybe polish it."

"This house does have some beautiful built-ins," he agreed. "And the trim work is flawless. Ray told me his father did all the finishing work."

"I'm so glad that you're familiar with this house," Debbie said. "I've known Ray my whole life from church, but I had never been in here before he called me and asked if I wanted to buy it."

"I heard that you're a Dennison native too. Strange that our paths didn't cross in such a small town. I must have graduated before you entered high school."

Debbie nodded. "My parents still live in the house where I was raised on the outskirts of town."

"Albright?" he asked. "Is that your married name?"

"My maiden name. Vance and Becca Albright are my parents."

His face lit up with recognition. "I play golf with Vance on Wednesday nights in Uhrichsville. He's a legend in the men's league over there."

Debbie smiled. "I'm not surprised to hear that. He's been a big golfer ever since I was a kid."

"Do you golf?"

She paused. "A little."

"That's what all the good golfers say." He chuckled and glanced around. "How about we discuss those guest rooms first? See if we can get them ready in time."

The basement steps were under the main floor stairway in the foyer. Debbie opened the door and flipped on the light. On their descent, she began, "Right now, these rooms are concrete floors and brick walls. I'd like to put up some drywall and lay down carpet. The windows also need to be updated and brought up to code. Some light fixtures will need to be put in as well."

"This sounds like a pretty big job."

She stopped at the bottom of the steps. "Do you think you'll have time?"

"Three weeks?" He scrunched up his eyes as he thought. "I'm finishing up a job right now, and I have another one lined up, but I might be able to push it off for a few weeks."

"I wouldn't want to inconvenience anyone else."

He shook his head. "It wouldn't be any trouble. It's not a pressing matter. Just something the owner wants done eventually. He's in no hurry."

The center of the basement would make a nice family room someday, but right now, Debbie was most concerned about the bedrooms. There was another bedroom on the second floor, but she planned to turn that into a home office. She wanted her guests to have a little more privacy, so they would use the basement bedrooms.

"It's a nice, dry basement," Greg commented as he rubbed Hammer's head. "I don't recall Ray ever complaining about water down here. We shouldn't have any trouble finishing it off."

Debbie showed him the two rooms she wanted turned into bedrooms. They wouldn't have closets, but she'd seen some shelving and hanging rods online that would work fine for her guests' needs. She could research that further and get something ordered.

"Do you think you can do it?" she asked. "In three weeks?"

"We'll have to get the carpet ordered right away," he said, "but I have a couple of guys I've worked with in the past, and I think they could squeeze it in." He gave her a cost estimate for the project, which she felt was reasonable. "I'll get started on Tuesday, if that's okay."

"That would be great." It was such a weight off Debbie's shoulders to have this project underway.

Her phone vibrated in her back pocket, and she pulled it out to see that Janet had texted her.

"I'll get some measurements," Greg said.

"Let me know if you need help. I'll just be a second."

As he started measuring, Debbie read the text and saw that Janet was at the café, working on some of her recipes and trying to get familiar with the new oven. She asked if Debbie could stop by and sample the muffins she had made.

After a quick text back telling her that she'd be there as soon as possible, Debbie looked up in time to see Greg struggling to get a measurement of the length of the room.

She laughed. "What, you haven't trained Hammer to hold the end of a tape measure yet?"

He straightened up, looking thoughtful. "Now there's an idea," he said. "He'll do just about anything for a treat."

"Here," she said, "let me help."

He smiled at her, revealing his dimples again, and in that moment Debbie knew that she was going to enjoy working with Greg Connor.

Thirty minutes later, after Debbie had finalized some initial plans with Greg, she headed to the café in the Dennison Depot on Center Street.

From what she recalled from her grandmother's stories, the town of Dennison had been established because it was both a hundred miles from Columbus and a hundred miles from Pittsburgh. In those days the trains needed their water supply replenished every hundred miles, so that made Dennison the perfect spot for a station. The Pittsburgh, Cincinnati & St. Louis Railway built the largest railroad yard in the country right there in Dennison in 1864, and the population boomed with the town growing up around the depot, which sat right in the middle.

By the time World War II broke out in 1941, the depot was a major stop on the Pennsylvania Railroad. Almost everyone in town knew the history of the depot during the war era, when it became a Salvation Army canteen run by four thousand active volunteers from eight counties, serving over 1,300,000 soldiers during the war.

But over the years, with the decline in railroading, the depot had fallen into disrepair until it was an eyesore in the community. The citizens started to rally around it in the 1980s to save it from being torn down like so many others in the Midwest. Now it was fully restored and housed a museum on one end and Debbie and Janet's renovated café on the other. If what Debbie's parents said was true, the whole community was excited that the café was opening again.

Debbie parked and then walked into the western end of the large depot where the Whistle Stop Café was located. In the weeks since Debbie and Janet had leased the space, they had cleaned, painted, and restored everything that was worth saving. The original booths had been in complete shambles, so they carried them to the dump and found tables and chairs from a café that was closing in Columbus. They had sent the chairs out to get reupholstered, and they were still waiting on those. They completely updated the kitchen, including a new stove, oven, and commercial-grade dishwasher.

As Debbie opened the door, the bell rang overhead, and she had to stop and take it all in. Just a few months ago, she'd been working a corporate job in Cleveland, living in an apartment downtown, juggling life in the city.

Now here she stood, co-owner of a café, living in a beautiful, historic home, back where she started.

It was still hard to believe some days, though she didn't have a single regret.

"There you are," Janet said as she came through the swinging door from the kitchen and into the spacious dining room. Large windows, freshly washed, allowed the afternoon sun to stream in from both sides of the room. The tall ceiling was covered in beautiful white tin, the plastered walls were painted a cheerful yellow with a deep red wainscotting, and the floors were a dark wood. Tables were sprinkled throughout the room, and a large counter and stools stretched across one side of the space.

Good. Dale had installed the stools.

"You're just in time to sample the muffins, hot out of the finicky oven." Janet wore an apron over her slacks and blouse, the same clothes she'd worn to church that morning. She usually wore jeans and fun T-shirts, most of them with bakery puns or sayings.

"Did you come over from church?" Debbie asked.

"Ian and Tiffany were going fishing this afternoon." Janet shrugged. Tiffany, Janet and Ian's daughter, had recently graduated from high school and would be heading off to college in Cleveland this fall. "So I thought I'd come over and work on some of my recipes." She frowned. "I'm not loving the new oven though. It heats faster on the left side, so some of these muffins are a little browner than I'd like."

Overcooked or not, they smelled delicious. Debbie took a nice long whiff.

"Don't the stools look great?" Janet asked.

"They do. Now we just need to finish the restrooms and get the chairs back from the upholsterer."

"Don't forget decorating." Janet motioned to the bare walls. They had both been on the lookout for WWII-era magazines, movie posters, and calendars to frame. With the connection to the canteen history, they wanted the café to have the look and feel of the 1940s.

"Here," Janet said, "try the raspberry cream cheese muffin first." She cut it in half with a butter knife. It fell open, and steam poured out.

"Mmm," Debbie said. "This is the real reason I wanted to open up a café with you. I get to sample all the food."

Janet smiled. She watched closely as Debbie pinched off a piece of the muffin and took a bite.

It melted in Debbie's mouth, sending the rich flavors dancing across her tongue.

"This is delicious," she said, nodding emphatically. "My favorite."

Janet laughed. "You haven't tried anything else yet," she said.

"I don't need to."

As Debbie sampled the others—blueberry, banana nut, cinnamon-swirl, double-fudge chocolate chip, and a lemon poppyseed—she told Janet about her visit with Ray.

"He said the record is from his long-lost sweetheart, Eleanor O'Reilly."

"Long-lost sweetheart?"

"They met just two weeks before he left for the war. She said she would wait for him to return, but when he got back to Dennison, she had disappeared, and no one knew where she had gone. He looked for her for months but never found her—and he never loved again."

Janet stared at Debbie. "Are you serious? How sad."

"He asked me if I would help him find her."

"What did you say?"

Debbie shrugged. "I said yes, of course. But I have no idea where to start. If he couldn't find her, how will I, eighty years later?"

"Maybe we can talk to some of the people who were here at the time. It's possible that she didn't want Ray to know where she was going and swore people to secrecy. So much time has passed, perhaps people are willing to talk now."

"I guess that's possible." Debbie took a bite of the cinnamon-swirl, loving it just as much as the other ones. "Who is still living in Dennison who was here eighty years ago?"

"I think Kim's mom is still living." Janet wiped her fingers on a napkin. "She might even be at the same retirement home as Mr. Zink. Her name is Eileen Palmer."

Kim Palmer Smith was the museum curator. She was working with Debbie and Janet as they restored the café, helping them with her knowledge of the depot and the history of Dennison.

"I think I remember Eileen," Debbie said, pulling some memories from the back of her mind. "She used to volunteer for the Christmas Train I took with my family every year as a child. I think she was the stationmaster at one point—maybe even during the war. She would ride the train with us at Christmas and share some of the history along the way."

"I remember that too." Janet smiled. "We should stop in and chat with Kim to see if her mom is up for visitors. Maybe Kim has some information that could help us too."

"It's worth a shot." Debbie was ready to talk to whomever necessary to find out what happened to Eleanor O'Reilly.

They finished up their muffin samples, and Debbie clasped her hands. "Well," she said, "I think it's official. All of these muffins need to be on the menu."

"All of them?" Janet asked. "I have about six others I want to try next."

Debbie shrugged. "We'll have to have a rotating muffin menu then. A few different ones each day. People will need to come in every day to see which muffins are being featured."

"That's a good idea." Janet popped the last piece of blueberry into her mouth. "I still need to finalize the rest of the bakery menu. I have so many choices, I can't seem to narrow them down."

"I think it's safe to say that no matter what you choose, our customers are in for a treat."

Janet grinned as she stood and cleaned up their leftovers.

As her friend disappeared back into the kitchen, Debbie gathered up her purse and made a mental note to visit with Kim in the morning. Hopefully she could point them in the right direction to find Eleanor O'Reilly.

Someone had to know what happened to her—didn't they?

Or was her history lost, like so many others from the Greatest Generation who had passed on?

# CHAPTER FOUR

On Monday morning, Debbie was awake with the sun, sorting boxes, hanging pictures, arranging furniture, and organizing drawers. She planned to work on her house in the morning and then at the café for the rest of the afternoon. When the café opened, she would need to be there at six every morning, but that was not this morning.

For now, she needed to focus on her house, and it was a big job. Though her parents, Janet, Ian, and Tiffany had been helpful over the weekend, there was still a lot to do. Even if she worked every morning for the next three weeks, she wasn't sure if she'd be ready for her friends' arrival. More than anything, Debbie wanted to show them that leaving her job in Cleveland and moving back to her hometown had been a good idea. She wanted everything to be perfect for their visit, including the house.

By lunchtime, Debbie was ready for a break, and Janet had asked her to come down to the café to sample a few more of her dishes. The contractor should be there, and Debbie was eager to ask him when the chairs were expected back from the upholsterer. They couldn't open a café without chairs.

Being at the café would also give Debbie a chance to see what Kim could tell her about Eleanor O'Reilly. Even though the museum was closed on Mondays, Kim was often there, and she had told Debbie and Janet they could stop in if they saw her car parked out front.

"It smells amazing in here!" Debbie said as she walked into the kitchen of the café at noon. "What are you making?"

"Chicken pot pie, roast beef, garlic mashed potatoes, and chicken dumpling soup." Janet grinned at Debbie. "What will you have first?"

"Everything."

As they sampled the delicious food, Debbie noticed how quiet the café was.

"Have you heard from Dale today?" she asked, and then took a bite of the steaming pot pie.

"Not a word." Janet shook her head. "I even called and asked about the chairs, but I got his voice mail, and he hasn't returned my call."

"He knows we open in less than three weeks," Debbie said, trying to reassure herself. "It'll come together."

"I hope you're right. It will be hard to open a café without a restroom if he doesn't get it finished."

"Or chairs," Debbie added.

Thirty minutes later, after the two friends had discussed each of the dishes and cleaned up their lunch, they headed over to the museum to see if Kim was available to talk.

The Dennison Railroad Depot Museum took up the bulk of the large building and provided a wonderful history of the old station. Kim was not only brilliant at her work, but she was always willing to chat and share her knowledge with Debbie and Janet.

"Hello," Kim called from her office. Her desk faced a window that allowed her to see anyone standing at the front counter. "What can I do for you?" she asked as she came out of her office to stand behind the counter.

"Hi, Kim. We were hoping you'd be able to answer some of our questions about a young woman who volunteered at the canteen in 1943," Debbie said.

"I can sure try." Kim smiled, and her brown eyes warmed. "But there were over four thousand volunteers who came and went in the war years, from eight surrounding counties. It might be hard to pinpoint just one of them."

"Her name was Eleanor O'Reilly," Debbie continued. "She was Raymond Zink's sweetheart, and she was supposed to wait for him to come home from the war, but when he got back to Dennison, she was gone and no one knew where she went."

"Eleanor O'Reilly." Kim said the name slowly, as if trying it on for size to see if it fit with anything she already knew. "If she was Ray's sweetheart, maybe she knew my mom. Ray and Mom have been friends since childhood, and my mom often mentions him when she talks about her days as a stationmaster. Ray worked for her for a little while before he left to fight."

"We were hoping your mom might be available to talk," Janet said. "Is she still living at Good Shepherd?"

"She is." Kim nodded. "And she'd love some visitors. Her mind is sharp, and she enjoys talking about the days when the depot was a thriving Salvation Army Canteen. Like I said, she was the stationmaster, but she also took it upon herself to keep an eye out for some of the younger volunteers who came to stay in Dennison. They were often teenage girls who wanted to be part of the war effort but didn't have family living in the area. They would board with some of the local residents."

"I believe Eleanor was one of those girls," Debbie said. "Ray told me that she boarded with a family by the name of Snodgrass, right across the road from his house—my house now."

"I know the name Snodgrass," Kim said with an enthusiastic smile. "They boarded several girls over the years the canteen was in operation."

"Are any of the Snodgrasses around?" Janet asked. "Perhaps we could talk to one of them."

"Not that I know of." Kim shook her head. "They had two sons who both fought in the war, which is probably why they opened their home to the volunteers. Unfortunately, neither of their sons made it back."

Sadness weighed on Debbie's heart as she thought about the great sacrifice so many families had given for their country.

"But," Kim said in a more positive tone, "my mom might know who Eleanor was. She knew several of the boarders, like I said, and she'd be happy to talk to you about them. If you have time this afternoon, I can see if she's available for visitors."

"That would be great." Debbie looked at Janet to see if she had other plans.

"This afternoon would be perfect," Janet agreed.

As Kim returned to her office to make the phone call, Debbie walked over to one of the beautiful stained-glass windows that allowed natural light to seep into the dark interior. The center pane was clear, but around the edges were rectangles of various-colored glass.

"Look," Debbie said to Janet as she pointed to the window. "Kim told me that the black paint along the edges of the glass was from the blackouts during the war. They left it here as part of the story of the building."

"It's an awesome piece of history," Janet said. "At first I wasn't sure if I had it in me to start a café with you, but the more time I spend in this building, the more I realize it was the best idea you've ever had."

"And I've had a lot." Debbie laughed, thinking of all the shenanigans she and Janet had gotten into over the years, growing up in Dennison together. They'd been best friends since grade school, and even after Debbie had left Dennison to live in Cleveland, they'd remained close. Opening up a café together, combining Debbie's business experience with Janet's cooking and baking skills, seemed like the perfect culmination of their friendship.

And who knew? Maybe their days of shenanigans weren't over. Maybe they were just getting started.

"I spoke to Mom," Kim said, leaving her office, "and she'd love to meet with you. She said to come on over whenever you're ready. And she actually knows more about Eleanor than I would have guessed, but I'll let her fill you in."

"Perfect," Debbie said. "Thank you so much."

"Just ask for Eileen Palmer when you get there, and they'll direct you to her room. She said she has a guest visiting right now, and she might be helpful too."

"Who's that?" Debbie asked.

"Susan Donlea. She's the daughter of Mabel Holman, one of my mom's old friends. From the stories I've heard, Mabel also worked at the canteen. Maybe Mabel mentioned Eleanor to Susan."

"We could only be so fortunate," Janet said. "From what Ray told us, no one knew a thing about Eleanor's disappearance."

"Maybe the women knew something Ray didn't," Kim suggested with a smile. "They often do." She pushed away from the counter. "I'll keep my eye out for you and see if I can find anything about Eleanor O'Reilly here at the depot. We have a research library, and sometimes I come across helpful things in there."

"Thank you," Debbie said. "Hopefully we all find something useful."

"Ray deserves to know what happened," Kim added. "I'll do what I can to make it possible."

As the women left the museum, Debbie hoped and prayed they were on the right path. Eleanor didn't just disappear off the face of the earth. Someone had to know the truth.

The Good Shepherd Retirement Center sat outside of town, on a gently rolling piece of property that boasted paved paths, a small pond, and benches positioned anywhere a person might want to rest and take in the view. Tall, majestic pine trees stood like sentinels around the building, offering shade and greenery throughout the year. Debbie used to enjoy going to work with her dad when he was the director. It was a peaceful place to visit, and she had always loved talking with the residents.

Debbie pulled up to the home not long after leaving the depot, her heart beating a little faster at the knowledge that Eileen might know what happened to Eleanor. But, if she did, why didn't she just tell Ray? Surely they knew each other. After all, they lived at the same facility. *Had* Ray ever asked Eileen about Eleanor? If not, why not?

Hopefully they would soon get some answers. Janet climbed from the passenger seat and joined her on the walkway.

"Debbie Albright?" an elderly woman said from one of the chairs on the front porch.

Brilliant brown eyes, full of merriment and intelligence, met Debbie's gaze.

"Eileen Palmer?" Debbie asked.

"The one and only." Eileen motioned for Debbie and Janet to come join her. "It's too nice to be inside today, so we thought we'd wait for you out here."

The sky was a dazzling shade of blue, with lazy white clouds floating overhead. It wasn't too hot, especially with the gentle breeze. A beautiful day to be outside.

"It's nice to meet you," Debbie said as she shook Eileen's thin hand. "This is my friend, Janet Shaw."

Janet shook Eileen's hand. "I'm happy to meet you."

"You too," Eileen said with a smile. "And this is my friend, Susan Donlea," she said as they all shook hands. "I've known Susan since the day she was born. She's a baby boomer. Her mother, Mabel Holman, was one of my dear friends."

Susan was easily in her sixties or seventies, with snow-white hair. Her fond smile was directed toward Eileen. "We go way back, don't we?"

"Susan stops by once in a while," Eileen said. "And it's a good thing she's here today. I heard that you two are looking for information about Eleanor O'Reilly. Susan might know a thing or two about her as well."

Susan nodded as Debbie and Janet took two of the seats near Eileen. They sat around a patio table with a red potted geranium in the center.

"Do you remember her?" Debbie asked Eileen.

"My, do I." Eileen shook her head, her short white curls moving gently. "I haven't heard that name in decades, though there was a time when her name was on everyone's lips. She was quite the popular thing around the canteen."

"Oh?" Debbie leaned forward. "Why was that?"

Eileen clasped her hands in front of her. "I first need to know why you want information about Eleanor."

Debbie glanced at Janet before answering. "I bought Raymond Zink's house and found a record in the attic that Eleanor gave him. When I brought it here, Ray told me that he never heard from Eleanor after he returned from the war and that he always wondered what happened to her. He asked me to help him find out."

"So," Eileen said slowly, "Ray's looking for Eleanor again."

"Do you remember when he looked for her the first time?" Janet asked.

"Of course I do. Everyone knew Ray was looking for her."

"And you don't know where she went?" Debbie asked.

Eileen leaned back in her chair, her gaze on a distant time and place as she shook her head. "I remember those days like they were yesterday. I recall the very moment I introduced Eleanor to Ray—it was right after he spilled pickle juice all over her."

They all laughed as Eileen smiled and told them the story. It was very similar to the one Ray had told Debbie.

"From the moment they met," Eileen said, "they were inseparable, though they only had two weeks together. But so many romances bloomed overnight in those days. There wasn't time for courting—people eloped all the time. Unfortunately, some lived to regret it."

"Marry in haste, repent at leisure." Susan repeated the old saying with a smile.

"But Ray and Eleanor didn't elope," Debbie said.

"No." Eileen shook her head. "But I think Ray would have. He was so moonstruck, you'd think she was the only girl to ever exist. But Eleanor loved him too, very much. He played the piano, and she sang for the canteen dances. And what a voice! Everyone who heard her knew that she was destined for bigger things. Sadly, Ray and Eleanor only performed together at three dances before he left, but those three were the best we ever had."

"And the canteen dances were to raise money for the food and supplies, right?" Janet asked.

"Yes, ma'am," Eileen said. "We seemed to never run out of supplies and donations, even though everyone rationed their own food." She paused, as if getting lost in her memories. "But I was talking about Ray and Eleanor, wasn't I? Every waking moment they were together, and we all knew it was love at first sight. It was actually something sweet to watch. Gave me hope for my own happily-ever-after."

"From all accounts," Debbie said, "it sounds like they were deeply in love. Why wasn't she waiting for him when he got back?"

Eileen frowned for a moment and then shook her head. "I don't know. She just up and left Dennison one day right after New Year's, about six months after Ray left for the army, without saying goodbye, and none of us knew where she went. I was worried about her, but she had no folks to check in with, and she didn't leave a forwarding address, so I had no idea where to even look."

"Some people thought she left to volunteer for the army," Susan said. "In either the Women's Army Auxiliary Corps or the WAVES."

"Did you know about Eleanor?" Debbie asked Susan.

"My mother spoke of her often, actually." Susan sighed. "She lived with guilt and regret about Eleanor for years."

Both Debbie and Janet sat up a little straighter.

"What do you mean?" Debbie asked. "Why would she have guilt and regret about Eleanor?"

"My mama was madly in love with Raymond Zink too—"

"I think a lot of girls were." Eileen chuckled, a sparkle in her own eye when she spoke of Ray.

"Apparently, he looked like Gregory Peck," Susan continued. "But, more than that, Mama said he was a 'mighty nice boy.'" She smiled. "The way Mama remembered it, she was about to tell Ray how she truly felt about him the very day that Eleanor came to town."

"How sad for her," Janet said. "Finally getting up the courage to admit you like someone—and then watching him fall in love with someone else."

"A stranger, no less," Susan said. "From that first day, everyone knew what was happening, and Mama decided she couldn't tell Ray the truth. But she wasn't too worried—at first. She heard Eleanor talking about becoming a famous singer one day, and she didn't think that Eleanor was going to stick around Dennison and wait for Ray. So she did what any lovestruck girl would do. She tried to convince Eleanor that she wasn't right for him. But whatever she did, it backfired, and Mama lived with guilt the rest of her life. I think she thought she was responsible for Eleanor leaving Ray."

"Did your mother ever tell Ray any of this?" Debbie asked. "When he returned, looking for Eleanor, I mean? Did she tell him what she knew?"

Susan shook her head. "No, and that was why she always felt so guilty. As far as I know, Mama went to her grave without telling Ray of her part in Eleanor's disappearance."

"Why wouldn't she tell him?" Janet asked.

"She was too ashamed. She truly believed Eleanor left because of her."

"*Did* she leave because of your mother?" Debbie asked. "Or was it something else that took her away from here?"

"I don't know." Susan shrugged. "All I know is what Mama told me."

Debbie leaned forward again, this time toward Susan. Whatever story she had to tell, Debbie believed it would give them more insight into what happened eighty years ago.

# CHAPTER FIVE

*June 18, 1943*

*The air was hot and sticky, and usually Mabel Thomas didn't mind, especially not on a Friday night during a canteen dance. But tonight was different. The entire week had been different. And it was all because of Eleanor O'Reilly.*

*"What has you down tonight, Mabel?" Eileen asked as she came up to the refreshment table.*

*Mabel fingered the sash of her pretty yellow dress, the one that almost always made Ray stop and take notice of her—until now. The only time he'd paid any attention to her this past week was when he'd accidentally run into her with the broom. Even then, he'd barely muttered a quick apology, because Eleanor had walked into the canteen. He'd absentmindedly handed the broom to Mabel to keep sweeping.*

She tried not to let the tears well in her eyes as she turned away from Eileen.

"Nothing more than usual," she said, sniffling. "We got a letter from my brother yesterday. His letters always seem to make Mama happy when they first come, and then she gets sad again, hoping, praying, and waiting for the next one."

It wasn't why Mabel was down, but it was a good excuse. Lots of girls cried about their brothers being away at war.

Eileen was one of Mabel's best friends, even if she was three years older. They were more like sisters, though Mabel never spoke to Eileen about Ray. Secretly, Mabel thought maybe Eileen had a crush on him too. Most of the girls in Dennison felt that way about him. There was something about him that made him attractive. It was more than his good looks, which he had in spades, and more than his confidence and easygoing nature. He was just good and kind and thoughtful. Ray was the type of guy any girl would want to bring home to her mom and dad, to make plans with, to build a life together.

Both girls looked toward the small makeshift stage in the corner of the train station lobby where they held the canteen dances. Ray was at the upright piano that had been loaned to the canteen when it first started the dances, and Eleanor stood behind the microphone. As Ray played "Boogie-Woogie Bugle Boy," he looked up at Eleanor with the most disgusting, lovesick expression Mabel had ever seen—only because it wasn't directed at her.

Truthfully, Ray looked more handsome than ever before. Being in love suited him.

Eleanor's song came to an end, and the room erupted in applause. No one was even dancing. They all just stared at her.

"Boy, can that girl sing," Eileen said as she shook her head and joined in the applause.

Mabel refused to clap.

Eileen must have noticed, because she turned to Mabel. "Don't you think so?"

Turning her back to Eileen under the pretense of getting more cups for the lemonade, Mabel shrugged a shoulder, feigning indifference. "I've heard better."

A locomotive whistle blew outside, sending everyone into motion. Another troop train had arrived, and they would need to serve the men during the short layover.

Mabel left the lemonade and took up her position at the magazine table. They had more than magazines available. There were Bibles, religious tracts, newspapers, novels, stationery, and health pamphlets. It was

Mabel's job to make sure the soldiers had access to whatever reading or writing material they might want or need. It wasn't an important job—it was actually not a job at all. The soldiers were quite capable of finding what they wanted on the table. She was simply a smiling face to make them feel welcome.

The train came to a halt while Ray and Eleanor started up the next song, "In the Mood," by the Glenn Miller Band with lyrics from the Andrews Sisters. They would continue to perform as the soldiers ate so they'd have a bit of entertainment while they waited for the train to refuel. Some of the soldiers might ask the volunteers to dance and, within twenty minutes, the servicemen would be off again, on their way to points east of Ohio.

Hundreds of soldiers poured off the train, streaming to the food table, grabbing sandwiches, apples, pickles, coffee, and cookies. A few of them trickled over to the reading materials, and Mabel forced herself to put a smile on her face for these men. Though her heart was breaking, she could smile for the next twenty minutes.

Most of them didn't even look at the volunteers. They just grabbed their food and headed toward the music. Eleanor's voice drew them in like moths to a flame. Several of them didn't even bother to eat their food. Instead, they stood there, staring at her with their mouths gaping open.

"Hello," said a friendly voice at Mabel's right side.

She startled and turned to find a tall young man in uniform. He looked fresh off the family farm, with short blond hair and smiling blue eyes. He couldn't have been more than eighteen or nineteen, a year or two older than she was.

"Hello," Mabel said. "Would you like some reading material, Soldier?"

"How about a letter or two from you while I'm overseas?"

Mabel smiled, since he didn't seem like the polished, suave sort. He was too innocent and homegrown to be a ladies' man.

"What's your name?" he asked.

"Mabel Thomas. What's yours?"

"Sam Holman. I'm coming from basic training, but I'm originally from New Philadelphia. What about you?"

"Right here in Dennison. Would you like something to read?"

"I'd rather talk to you."

The noise in the canteen intensified as more soldiers got off the train. It was almost hard to hear

Eleanor's voice from where Mabel stood now. The platform was thick with servicemen and women.

They pushed and jostled around Sam, but he didn't let anyone or anything budge him.

"Wouldn't you rather go in and listen to the singing?" Mabel asked him. "Everyone else seems to be heading that way."

Sam shrugged, and Mabel noticed the spray of freckles across his nose. "I've heard people sing before, but I've never met you. I'd rather spend my time getting to know you better."

"You are smooth, Sam Holman," Mabel said, her shyness starting to creep up on her. "But if you're from New Philadelphia, then maybe you've heard our singer before. Her name is Eleanor O'Reilly."

Sam took notice of the name and looked toward the lobby, where the wide doors were open with a good view of the stage.

"Eleanor?" he asked with a frown. "That girl's the quietest, shyest thing in town. She's singing?"

"You know her then?"

"Sure, I know her. Went to school with her all my life."

Mabel suddenly wanted to talk to Sam. If he knew something about Eleanor that might turn Ray away from her, she needed to know. There had to be something *from her past that could be useful.*

"Do you like to dance, Sam?" Mabel asked.

He turned back to her and grinned, the tips of his ears turning red. "With you?"

She nodded.

"Okay." He offered her his hand and pushed his way through the crowd. He was taller than almost all the other men, and they moved out of his way.

There wasn't much space to dance, since hundreds of soldiers had come in to hear Eleanor sing.

For the first time in a week, Ray wasn't mooning over Eleanor. He was too busy glaring at all the servicemen who were gawking at his girl.

Good. At least he was getting a taste of how Mabel had felt this past week. Except that Eleanor wasn't gawking back at the soldiers. She looked shy and a little bashful at all the attention, but she kept on singing her heart out.

All the men were mesmerized—all of them except Sam. He smiled down at Mabel as if she were the only woman in the room.

Eleanor's voice filled the lobby.

"You're the prettiest girl I've ever met, Mabel Thomas," Sam said. "I meant it when I asked you to write to me. Will you?"

*"You're a fast-talker," Mabel teased.*

*"I only have fifteen minutes left to convince you to write to me. I don't have time to move slow."*

*For his size, Sam was a surprisingly good dancer. He was fast, light on his feet, and confident.*

*Mabel only had fifteen minutes left to find out all she could about Eleanor, so she decided not to waste any time. "You said you knew Eleanor?"*

*"Sure. We went to school together."*

*"What do you know about her? I heard she's an orphan?"*

*"I don't want to talk about her," he said. "I'd rather talk about you."*

*Mabel tried not to feel irritated. "There's nothing much to say. I live here in Dennison with my parents and my younger sister. My brother is fighting in Europe somewhere, and I volunteer here at the canteen seven days a week. That's about it."*

*"That's not all." He shook his head and smiled. "I know that behind those pretty green eyes there's an intelligent, funny, and kindhearted girl. I want to know your hopes and dreams, your fears and worries."*

*Mabel's gaze slid to Ray of its own accord. Her hopes and dreams? They were mingled with her biggest fears and worries right now. She longed for Ray to* love her, but she was afraid that if he didn't by now, he never would.

Sam's gaze followed hers, and he stiffened. "Do you belong to another guy, Mabel?"

She snapped her attention back to Sam. "I don't belong to anyone."

"Are you his girl?" He tilted his head toward Ray.

"Eleanor's his girl," she said bitterly. "He hasn't noticed anyone or anything since the day she arrived."

"I see how it is." He didn't relax but tightened his hold on Mabel just a little. "Is that why you want to know about Eleanor?"

"It can't hurt to know who came in and stole Ray away from the rest of us."

Sam was quiet for a moment, and then he said, "I'm going to write to you, Mabel Thomas, and I'm going to convince you that there's only one man on this planet for you—and that's me."

For the first time since they'd met, she focused her entire attention on Sam Holman. He wasn't a handsome man, but he wasn't ugly either. There was something wholesome and good in his eyes—but he lacked the charismatic, magnetic charm that Ray had. She'd always loved Raymond Zink, and the thought that she could ever love someone else felt strange and unnatural.

"You can try," she finally said with a sigh. "But I don't think I'll ever love anyone like I love Ray."

"Challenge accepted." He swung her around so his back was to Ray and she couldn't see over his shoulder. The entire stage was blocked from her view.

But she could still hear Eleanor.

It was midnight and time to close up the canteen. They'd be open again in four hours, but another team of volunteers was coming in from Port Washington, and Mabel would be sleeping.

She should be tired now, but ever since she'd danced with Sam, she'd felt energized. After she gave him her address, she waved him off, watching his train disappear down the tracks, wondering if she'd ever hear from him again.

It felt funny that, after seeing off countless other troop trains, her brother's included, this one was the one that she felt the most connected to—and all because of Sam Holman. A stranger she had spent exactly seventeen minutes with.

Eleanor and Ray put away the microphone, wrapped up the cord, and then pushed the piano back to the wall, talking quietly together the entire time.

Jealously and resentment rose up in Mabel as she forgot all about Sam Holman and remembered why she'd been so upset this past week.

Sam hadn't been helpful. All he had told Mabel was that Eleanor was an orphan who lived with a grumpy older couple on a farm outside New Philadelphia. She hadn't gone around with a crowd like all the other kids but had been stuck at the farm. She didn't have a lot of friends, didn't go to any social gatherings, and didn't do much outside of school and church.

There was nothing about Eleanor that Mabel could use against her.

Maybe she needed to talk to Eleanor to find out what was wrong with her. There had to be something.

"Good night," Mabel said to Eileen as she left the canteen. "I'll see you tomorrow."

"Good night, Mabel," Eileen said. "Do you want me to walk home with you?"

The streets of Dennison were dark, but Mabel wasn't afraid to walk home by herself. Nothing good or bad happened in Dennison after all the boys left to fight in the war.

*"I'll be fine, thanks." Mabel left the depot and walked to the other side of the street. She planned to wait for Eleanor and join her on her way back to the Snodgrass house. Maybe she'd get a chance to ask her some pointed questions about her past.*

*After a few minutes, Eleanor and Ray came out of the depot together, hand in hand, their heads bent toward each other.*

*Mabel had to look away.*

*It was dark, so they probably couldn't see her standing there. As they moved away from the depot lighting, they too were swallowed up in the darkness.*

*Mabel wanted to talk to Eleanor, so she decided to follow them. When Ray left Eleanor at the Snodgrass house, Mabel could get her attention and talk to her then.*

*They took their time on their way home, and Mabel felt silly, slinking around behind them, trying not to be noticed. If they saw her this far away from her own home, they'd know she was following them.*

*There was nothing else moving at this time of night. It was so quiet, and the wind was so still, Mabel was able to catch some of their sugary-sweet words. It just made her madder.*

*As her eyes adjusted and the clouds moved out of the way, allowing the full moon to shed more light* on the street, Mabel was able to see a lot more than before.

Finally, when Ray and Eleanor got to the Snodgrass house, they stopped on the front stoop and faced each other.

Mabel stood on the opposite side of the road, behind a tree, but peeked out at them to see when Ray would leave.

They stood, face-to-face, holding hands.

"I'm going to be leaving next week," Ray said, his voice heavy. "I don't know how long it will be until I see you again."

"The war won't last much longer," Eleanor tried to reassure him. "We'll be together again sooner than you think."

"I hope you're right—but in case you're not, I want to know if you'll marry me, Eleanor. Before I leave."

Mabel held her breath, forcing herself not to call out for them to stop this nonsense.

"I love you," Ray continued, "and even though we've only been together for a week, when you know, you know."

"I don't think it would be a good idea, Ray. I love you too, and there's nothing that could make me fall out of love with you. I promise I'll wait for you, and we can be married as soon as you come home. Won't that be so much better? We can start our lives together, without the war hanging over our heads."

He looked down at their clasped hands and sighed. "You're right—but you have to promise me you'll wait for me."

Eleanor put her hand up to his cheek. "I promise, Ray."

And then, Raymond Zink kissed Eleanor O'Reilly. Right there, in front of Mabel.

Tears pricked her eyes, and she had to look away.

Finally, she chanced another look. Ray walked down the steps, holding on to Eleanor's hand until the very last second, and then he crossed the street and went into his own house.

Eleanor stood for a few moments to watch him, and when she was about to turn into her own house, Mabel called out to her.

"Eleanor!" She said it in a yelled whisper—wanting to attract her attention but no one else's.

Eleanor pivoted, surprise on her face.

Mabel quickly wiped away her tears and sprinted across the road. She didn't care whether or not Eleanor liked her. She didn't care if she hurt or insulted this stranger who had turned her world upside down. All she cared about was having Ray to herself.

"Mabel?" Eleanor asked. "What are you doing here?"

"I came to talk to you about Ray." Mabel was usually shy and reserved but not now, not when it mattered the most.

"Ray? You just missed him."

"No." Mabel lifted her chin. "I want to talk to you about Ray."

"What about Ray?" Eleanor frowned.

It was now or never, so Mabel took a deep breath. "You don't deserve him."

Eleanor's mouth dropped open, and she took a step back.

"I've known Ray my whole life," Mabel continued. "He's a part of Dennison, just like I'm a part of Dennison. You're not from around here. You're an outsider. I was here first. I've been in love with Ray since the first day of first grade—I was going to tell him too, the day you came."

Eleanor seemed to gather her wits about her, and she straightened. "I think Ray should be the one who determines who is right for him. And he chose me. You had all these years to win him over, but you didn't."

Mabel hated Eleanor in that moment, but she would never admit that Eleanor spoke the truth. "All you want is to be a singer. You'll go off to New York, or wherever, and forget about him. Ray belongs here in Dennison. He deserves to have a wife who will devote her entire life to him. That's not you, and you know it. Break it off now, before he leaves, so I have time to be the person he needs."

Eleanor frowned, her jaw tightening. "You don't know what I want."

"It's not hard to figure out."

As if realizing she didn't owe Mabel an explanation, Eleanor tilted up her chin and looked down her nose. "I don't need to talk to you about this. My life— and Ray's—are none of your business. I love Ray, and I won't break it off with him. I'll wait for him until he returns from the war, and then we'll go off to New York together. He told me that's what he wants. You don't know him as well as you think you do."

"That's where you're wrong. He only told you that because you've bewitched him. The real Ray wants to stay in Dennison, and I'll be here for him when you break his heart. You're not good enough for him, and he knows it. Maybe not now, but one day he'll realize it, and that's when I'll be waiting for him to come to me."

Eleanor stared at Mabel for several seconds, and then she simply opened the front door and walked into the house, leaving Mabel steaming on the front stoop.

*Slowly, Mabel turned and walked down the street, replaying every word in her head.*

*Maybe it had been enough. Maybe Eleanor would think about what she had heard and let Ray go.*

*It was the only hope Mabel had.*

## CHAPTER SIX

On Tuesday morning, Debbie allowed herself to enjoy a cup of coffee and a bagel as she did her devotions at the small table in the kitchen. Greg Connor was due any minute, and she wasn't sure if she'd have much time to herself for the rest of the day. She planned to head to the café after lunch, just like the day before, and that evening her parents were coming back to her house to help her unpack more boxes. It would be another full day, but Debbie was ready to tackle whatever was needed.

The doorbell rang a few minutes later, and she closed her Bible and ate the last bite of her bagel.

She had to move around several boxes as she went to the foyer and opened the front door.

Greg stood there with Hammer and two teenage boys just behind him. There was no mistaking that they were his sons. They both had his thick dark hair and brilliant blue eyes.

"Good morning," Debbie said.

"Hi." Greg's smile was wide as he motioned for his two boys to step forward. "I brought some help today so we could make as much headway as possible. This is Jaxon." He put his hand on the shoulder of the taller boy. "He'll be a freshman at the high school this year."

"Hello, Jaxon," Debbie said, smiling at the handsome young man. It was easy to picture what Greg might have looked like at that age.

"Hello," Jaxon said.

"And this," Greg said, putting his hand on the younger boy's shoulder, "is Julian. He'll be in seventh grade this fall."

"Hi, Julian," Debbie said. "It's nice to meet you."

"You too," Julian said with a shy smile, revealing dimples that matched his dad's. Thick freckles covered his boyish face, and his hair was a little longer, curling at the ends.

"Today we're going to frame up the walls in the bedrooms and start running the wiring," Greg said. "Hopefully we'll be ready to hang drywall in a day or two. Based on what you told me you're looking for, I have some carpet swatches for you to choose from. As soon as you do, I'll put a call in to my carpet guy and see if we can get the installation scheduled."

"I hope I'm not keeping you from your other jobs," Debbie said.

"I have a team of guys working on another project today." Greg adjusted the tool belt he had hitched over his shoulder. "We're all yours."

Debbie couldn't hide her smile. "Great. I'm willing to help—as long as I'm not in your way. Tell me what to do."

"We'll start by bringing in some supplies." He handed his tool belt to Jaxon. "Go ahead and take everything down to the basement," he said. "I'll get the miter saw and air tank set up out front." He turned to Julian. "Why don't you grab the nail gun and air hose out of the back of the truck. Make sure there are plenty of nails."

Julian nodded and then left the house to do his father's bidding.

Both of the boys were out of earshot, so Debbie said, "They look like capable young men. Do they work with you often?"

"As much as they can. They love helping. Jaxon is saving money to buy a car, and Julian wants a really expensive pair of basketball shoes." He shook his head, clearly not understanding how someone could spend so much money on shoes. "They both play baseball, so they can only help a few days a week. I hope you don't mind."

"Mind?" Debbie frowned. "Of course not. I'm happy they're here."

Greg smiled, revealing his dimples. "Thanks. Hopefully we'll be able to get a lot done today." He put his hand on Hammer's head. "Come on, boy. Let's get to work."

Debbie marveled at how well the three of them worked together. The boys seemed to anticipate Greg's needs before he asked and, within an hour, they were already working on the second wall of the first room. Since three of the four walls in each room were made of bricks, they had to frame them with two-by-fours before putting up the drywall.

Each time Greg called out a measurement, Jaxon went to the miter saw in the front yard and cut a two-by-four, which he brought back to the basement. Then Julian would hold it in place while Greg secured it with the large nail gun. Every once in a while, the air tank would kick on and refill with air. It was loud, but it was outside and didn't penetrate the thick walls in the basement. Debbie only heard it when she was upstairs or outside, helping haul more two-by-fours out of the trailer attached to Greg's truck.

After a couple of hours, Debbie made some lemonade and invited Greg and his boys to take a quick break. They came into the kitchen, where she had some cookies out on a tray for them. She set a big bowl of water on the floor for Hammer.

After washing up, the boys both grabbed a few cookies and a glass of lemonade and decided to sit out on the back stoop in the sunshine to fool with their phones. Hammer decided he needed to nose around in the grass for a while.

Greg stayed in the kitchen with Debbie. They both took a seat at her small table where the Bible lay.

"Do you like the progress you're making down there?" Debbie asked.

He nodded and set his lemonade down. "We're making good time. Did you choose a carpet option?"

"I did." Debbie stood, retrieved the swatches, and showed him which one she liked best.

"Great. I'll call my carpet guy as soon as we're done with our break." He took a bite of the cookie. "This is delicious. Did you make it?"

"Janet made it at the café." The chocolate chip cookie was soft and chewy. "It'll be available there when we open."

"Mmm." He took another bite, clearly enjoying it. "I'll have to stop by often."

"I hope you do—I hope everyone does."

"If the rest of the food is anything like this, I don't think you'll have trouble getting customers."

"I'm counting on it. I've staked everything on this venture. My friends in Cleveland think I'm foolish for taking the risk."

"Everything worth doing is worth some risk. The depot museum draws a big crowd every year, and the new bed-and-breakfast they're opening in the Pullman cars will help."

Someone had purchased a few sleeping cars and remodeled them. The cars were on unused railroad tracks near the depot and were supposed to be open by the end of the month to guests. Hopefully it would bring customers to the café.

"I'm thankful that Dennison is preserving the depot," Greg continued. "It's one of the most important buildings in town. The history of the Salvation Army Canteen should never be forgotten."

"Are you familiar with the history of the building?" Debbie took a sip of her lemonade.

"Very familiar with it. My grandmother was one of the volunteers who worked in the canteen even though she was a young mother, on a farm, when my grandfather left for the war. She was pregnant with my dad at the time, but she still showed up, once a week, to do her part. She stretched her own rations to donate sugar cookies to the canteen too. They were my grandfather's favorite, and she did it in his honor."

"I can't imagine." Debbie shook her head. "We have the benefit of knowing how the war ended, but they had no idea at that time. The worry that their loved ones would never return, having no idea how long the war would last, or if the good guys would even win. It's just incomprehensible."

"My grandfather didn't return," Greg said quietly. "He was killed in battle less than a year after he left, leaving my grandmother a widow with four children."

"I'm so sorry."

"At the end of the war, my grandfather's best friend returned from fighting and volunteered to help my grandmother on the farm.

They eventually fell in love and married." Greg smiled, tenderness softening his expression. "He was a wonderful husband and father, and they went on to have three more children together. I remember him from when I was a kid, but he died when I was in high school."

Debbie matched Greg's smile with one of her own. "I'm glad your grandmother's story had a happy ending."

"Me too." He finished off his cookie. "If you ever want to know more about the history of the depot, I'd be happy to tell you what I know. Kim Smith is great, but if she's not available, I'm always here. I don't know everything, but I know quite a bit."

There was something good and honest about Greg that Debbie admired. They'd only spent a few hours in each other's company, but she felt as if she'd known him for years. There was a level of comfort with him that she leaned into. Perhaps it was because they'd both grown up in Dennison and had known the same people—even if they hadn't known each other. Or maybe it was their shared love of history and the Dennison depot. Or maybe it was because he had such earnest, kind eyes and was easy to talk to.

Whatever it was, she looked forward to spending more time in Greg's company, getting to know both him and his sons.

"Maybe you can help me now," she said. "I promised Ray that I would look for a woman he met in 1943. Her name was Eleanor O'Reilly. She worked at the canteen for a few months, and then he never heard from her again—even though she promised to wait for him."

"I remember him talking about her a few times," Greg said. "He told me she had the voice of an angel and was the prettiest girl he'd ever met. When she wasn't here, waiting for him like she promised, it almost destroyed him. I'm pretty sure it's the reason he never married."

Debbie could understand that. After her fiancé, Reed, died, she thought she would never recover. The idea of loving someone again—of opening her heart to the possibility of that kind of pain—was still something she couldn't fathom. No wonder Ray never married.

"Do you have any idea what might have happened to her?" Debbie asked.

He shook his head. "I have no idea. Other than hearing Ray talk about her, I've never heard of her." He paused and frowned as he seemed to think of something. "But there might be someone else who has. Have you met Harry Franklin?"

"I don't believe I have."

Greg's face lit up. "You'll love Harry. He was fifteen when he started working as a porter at the depot during the war. He knew everything about everyone and has one of the sharpest memories around. I'm surprised you haven't met him yet. He often likes to sit at the depot with his dog, Crosby, and watch the trains go by."

"I've been so busy whenever I've been at the depot. I might have seen him, but I haven't had the chance to meet everyone yet."

"When you do, be sure to ask him about Eleanor. He might have an idea of what happened to her."

The boys entered the kitchen just then, asking for more lemonade and cookies. Debbie jumped up to get them, excited that she'd uncovered another possible source of information about Eleanor's disappearance.

Debbie left Greg, Hammer, and the boys at her house after lunch and headed to the depot. Janet was stopping by a local gallery to pick up some posters they'd had framed, which gave Debbie a little time to see if she could find Harry Franklin before rendezvousing with her friend at the café.

When she got to the depot, she looked around outside and saw an elderly, distinguished-looking African American gentleman with a white dog at his side. The dog sat up when he saw Debbie, instantly going on the alert. There was a circle of black fur around his right eye, with smaller specks of black covering his body.

The man was portly around the middle, and his white hair and eyebrows were a stark contrast to his smooth, dark skin. He sat on a bench with one hand on the dog's head until Debbie appeared in his view. As soon as he saw her, he sat up a little straighter and began to stand.

"Don't get up on my account," Debbie said as she approached him. "Though I appreciate the gallantry."

Harry settled back to the comfort of his seat, a wide smile on his face. He tipped his cap. "There was a time when I'd have jumped off this bench at the sight of a pretty lady, but my arthritic joints aren't as dependable as they once were. I haven't jumped in years."

"Are you Harry Franklin?" Debbie asked.

"Yes, ma'am." He extended his hand. "And you must be Debbie Albright. I've heard all about you, and I've seen you from a distance. I'm planning to be your first customer when the café opens."

Debbie shook hands with Harry and smiled. "Thank you. I look forward to having you at the café. But please don't wait until we open. Stop by any time."

"I think I might do that. Care to join me for a spell?" Harry glanced at his watch. "Another train is due past here in about five minutes. This entire area used to be covered in tracks, almost as far as you could see. Now we just have the one set." He shook his head and sighed. "Time marches on."

"It does do that." She took a seat at Harry's side.

"This here is Crosby," Harry said, petting the dog.

"Hello, Crosby." Debbie held her hand out for Crosby to sniff. "He's a handsome dog."

"Descended from a dog named Bing, one of the most famous military veterans from Dennison."

"I've heard of Bing," Debbie said as she scratched Crosby's head. "I heard more of his story just the other day."

"Did you hear that Bing's cape and helmet are in the museum?"

"I've seen them," Debbie said warmly. "And Crosby is one of his descendants?"

"Sure is." Harry's voice was filled with pride.

"I heard you worked as a porter here during World War II," Debbie said. "And that you knew everything about everyone."

Harry grinned. "Well, now, I can't say that latter part is completely true. But I did know my way around this place." He looked at the depot with fondness. "I don't think there was ever a man who enjoyed his work as much as I did. I continued my career with the railroad and retired almost thirty years ago already. I loved every minute of it, but nothing was as special as working here during the war, when the canteen was in full swing."

Debbie could almost imagine it with him. She felt a similar sense of pride and accomplishment as Harry when she thought about her café. "This building has brought a lot of happiness to a lot of people."

"Ain't that the truth." Harry's chuckle was contagious, and Debbie found herself joining him. Slowly, his smile faded. "But it brought a lot of sadness too." His attention was stolen as he leaned forward, looking down the track. "Here she comes. A couple of minutes early."

A train moved toward Dennison from the west, coming fast. The sound of railroad crossing bells went off, and the lights at the nearest crossing started to flash. Soon the train was flying by so loudly that it didn't pay to talk. The wind from the train fluttered Debbie's hair, teasing and tickling her cheeks.

It took a few minutes for it to pass, but when it finally did, Harry said, "It never gets old. Now, what can I do for you, Miss Debbie? I don't think you stopped by just to visit with an old man and his dog."

"I actually did come with a question I was hoping you could answer."

"Ask away." He crossed his arms, looking like he was getting comfortable. "Crosby and I will see if we can answer it."

She smiled again and then said, "Do you remember a young woman by the name of Eleanor O'Reilly? She would have been a volunteer at the canteen in the summer of 1943. I'm asking for Raymond Zink. He said she was supposed to be waiting for him when he returned to Dennison, but she wasn't. And he never heard from her again."

Harry's face fell at the name, and he looked down at his lap. "Eleanor O'Reilly."

"You knew her?"

"Everyone knew her. At least, we knew who she was." His face filled with excitement. "What a looker! And that voice? Never heard anything like it before or since. She was something special, all right."

"Do you remember what happened to her?"

Harry looked away and fidgeted. Was he uncomfortable talking about Eleanor?

"I've always had a suspicion about what happened to her," he finally said, "but I can't say for sure."

Debbie leaned forward. "What do you think happened to her?"

Harry lifted his gaze and looked out at the train yard, as if he were seeing a different time and place. "I'll tell you what I think happened, but you can't tell Ray."

His response took Debbie by surprise. "Why not?"

"Ray has been a friend since we both worked at the depot together, and if he knew what I did, he would never forgive me." He glanced at Debbie quickly, almost defensively. "But keep in mind that what I did, I thought I was doing for him. I never would have done it if I knew Eleanor was going to run off and not wait for him."

"I promised Ray I would help him find Eleanor," Debbie said, feeling her hopes deflate. "I can't keep information from him, especially if it tells us what happened to her."

Harry studied Debbie with his dark eyes. Though he was old, he still had the spark of youth in his gaze. "Well, the truth is, I don't know if it will be helpful. But if we can find answers, maybe it can give him closure."

# CHAPTER SEVEN

*June 25, 1943*

*Harry Franklin couldn't help but tap his foot to the sound of the music as he loaded luggage onto the passenger car. The train had stopped at the Dennison depot that Friday evening on its way east.*

*"Who is that singing?" a passenger asked him as she reached into her purse and pulled out a coin to tip him. Even though it was a warm evening, she wore a mink stole around her shoulders.*

*Accepting the money, Harry tapped his hat and nodded at her. "That's Miss Eleanor O'Reilly, ma'am."*

*"Is she a famous singer?" the woman asked.*

*"Famous around here—but nowhere else, I reckon." Harry grinned. "Not yet, anyway."*

*The woman stood on the steps of the train, looking toward the depot where the doors and windows were wide open. "It's the weekly canteen dance," Harry said.*

"It's a fundraiser to help feed the service members who come through on troop trains."

"My son is serving," the woman said as she opened her purse one more time. She pulled out a twenty-dollar bill and pressed it into Harry's white-gloved hand. "Would you please give this to the ladies in the canteen?" Tears glistened in her eyes. "I just hope and pray that my son is receiving such a warm welcome wherever he is right now."

"Yes, ma'am. Thank you." Harry tapped his hat again as the lady entered the passenger train and disappeared.

Harry looked at the bill in his hand. It wasn't often that he saw such a large amount of money, especially since the war had started. The donation would go a long way in helping the ladies with the canteen. He couldn't wait to see what Eileen had to say.

"All aboard," the conductor called as he hung off one set of stairs, looking left and right for passengers.

A couple of men in dark suits and fedoras ran out of the depot and moved past Harry to climb on board.

"That young lady has a great career ahead of her," one of the men said.

"If I knew I could grab another train and not be stuck in the middle of Ohio," said the second, "I'd stay and convince her to come to New York City to audition for a record label."

"It would take a lot of convincing," said the first. "She seems a bit of a greenhorn."

"Nothing that an agent couldn't handle. When you've got what it takes, it's easy to fix the rest...." Their conversation faded away as they got into the passenger car.

Harry headed back toward the depot with the men's conversation rolling through his mind. Eleanor sure did have a pretty voice. What if those men were music producers? And what might have happened if they had taken the time to talk to Eleanor? Were they right? Did she have what it took to become a famous singer?

Harry sure thought so.

"Miss Eileen." Harry approached the stationmaster where she was replenishing the refreshment table. She always seemed to be easy to find in the depot, morning, noon, and night, rarely taking a day off. And even when she did have a day off, she usually volunteered in the canteen.

"Hello, Harry," Eileen said. "Did the train get off?"

"Yes, ma'am." Harry was fifteen, and though Eileen was just five years older, he treated her with the respect he'd give to any boss, be it man or woman, five, ten, or twenty years older than he was. "And we got a donation from one of the passengers. She wants it to go to the canteen."

He handed the twenty-dollar bill to Eileen and watched as her eyes lit up with surprise. "How generous. Did you get her name?"

"No. But she heard Eleanor singing. When I told her about the fundraiser, she pulled out the money and said she had a son who was serving and that she hoped he was being treated with the same warm welcome wherever he was tonight."

"Thank you, Harry. I'll see that this money is put to good use." She slipped the bill into her pocket and then glanced at her wristwatch. "It's getting late, and your shift was over thirty minutes ago. Why don't you go on home?"

"I think I'll stay and listen for a while, if that's okay," Harry said. "Tonight's Ray's last night. He's leaving in the morning, isn't he?"

Sadness glinted in Eileen's gaze as she nodded. "He'll be leaving on the eight o'clock train."

Eleanor began to sing "I'll Be Seeing You." The sweet, gentle song made everyone slow down and stare at her. But she didn't look at her audience. She stared at Ray, and he at her.

Harry knew that tonight was the last time they would play and sing together until the war was over.

He looked around and saw that many of the volunteers working at the canteen must be thinking of their own husbands, sons, brothers, and sweethearts who were already gone as they listened, because they were wiping their eyes.

Harry swallowed his own emotions, wishing he had the power to call off the war and bring back all the loved ones who had already left to fight. He wished he could prevent Ray from going tomorrow too. And, more than anything, he wished he was old enough to go himself.

He was so caught up in the song that, when it came to an end, it felt like he'd been mesmerized, and it took a moment for him to snap out of the daze he was in.

There was a pause as Eleanor collected her emotions, and then she nodded at Ray, whose hands were poised over the piano.

"I'd like to dedicate this last song to Ray," Eleanor said as she spoke into the microphone. "And please join me in praying for him and all the others serving. May God bless them and bring them home soon."

Ray looked away and wiped his face.

Harry pulled out a handkerchief and had to wipe his own eyes. He'd watched plenty of his friends, family, and neighbors march off to war, and it never got easier.

Soon Ray was playing the last song, "Under the Apple Tree" by the Andrews Sisters. Eleanor sang it often, but she did it so well, no one complained about hearing it again.

The song was easy to sing along with, and almost everyone joined Eleanor for the last chorus.

When it came to an end, Eleanor went to her coat, which lay on a chair, and removed a record from underneath. She motioned for Ray to join her at the microphone.

"What's this?" Ray asked as Eleanor handed him the record.

"I had it made," she said with a bright smile. "It's a recording of me singing 'Under the Apple Tree' so you can listen to it whenever you start to miss me."

Ray looked down at Eleanor and shook his head. "I'll wear it out."

Harry could see that Ray wanted to kiss his girl, but—

"One more round of applause for Miss Eleanor O'Reilly," Ray finally said into the microphone.

The room erupted with applause, and Eleanor's cheeks deepened into a pretty pink. As the clapping died down, people started to walk up to the stage to say goodbye to Ray and to wish him well.

*Eleanor stood back, watching quietly, tears glistening in her eyes.*

*As Harry studied them, thinking about how war tore people apart, he was happy that Ray could at least have something to carry with him from Eleanor. That record was a priceless gift, one he was sure Ray would guard with his life.*

*Harry's gaze slipped to the record, and an idea began to form. His thoughts turned to those men in the dark suits and what they had said about Eleanor's singing as they got onto the train. Could Eleanor really make it in New York City? Would there be a record company that liked her singing enough to pay her to make records?*

*The idea grew in Harry's mind, and the more he considered it, the more he liked it.*

*Excitement filled his chest, and he lifted his chin, grinning.*

*He'd thought of a way to help both Eleanor and Ray—as long as he could get Eleanor to agree with his plan.*

*Even if he couldn't, he'd still find a way to carry it out.*

*With all the happiness that Eleanor and Ray's music had brought to the service members, the volunteers, and the passengers who came through the depot these past couple of weeks, they deserved some happiness too. And Harry was going to see that they got it.*

*The day Ray left Dennison was one of the saddest days Harry could remember. He'd only been working as a porter for two months, but in that time, he'd become good friends with Ray. They'd worked well together, and, until Eleanor had arrived, they'd spent a lot of time together too.*

*But Harry didn't mind that he hadn't seen Ray as much lately. He didn't blame him for going all mushy and spending all his waking moments with Eleanor. Instead, Harry looked forward to the day when he would fall in love too. If Harry had a sweetheart as wonderful as Eleanor, he knew he'd be acting the same way.*

*But the hour had finally arrived for Ray to leave. He had turned eighteen just three days ago, and he'd volunteered to serve as an infantryman in the United States Armed Services. He'd been busy in the past few days preparing to leave, but now there was nothing left to do but say goodbye.*

*His mother, father, and little sister were all at the station, along with Eleanor, Eileen, Mabel, and others. Ray was a popular young man, so Harry wasn't surprised to see so many people there to say goodbye to him. Ray's mother cried into a handkerchief, his father tilted his chin up in a stoic gesture, and his little sister clung to his waist.*

*Ray looked fine in his suit, his hair cut short and his face shining. But Harry could see apprehension and worry in his gaze. Ray was being patriotic and courageous, but that didn't mean he wasn't afraid.*

*Eleanor also cried into a handkerchief as Ray said goodbye to his parents, his sister, his friends, his coworkers, his neighbors, and everyone else who came out to wish him well.*

*"All aboard," called the conductor as the steam released from the locomotive.*

*"That's me," Ray said. His gaze caught on Harry. He grinned and waved him over. "Harry! I can't leave without saying goodbye to you."*

*The others made a path for him, and Harry walked up to Ray. He extended his hand, but Ray pulled Harry into a tight bear hug.*

*"Make sure the depot runs smoothly while I'm gone," Ray said with a chuckle.*

"I sure will," Harry said. "You come home as soon as you can."

"I'll do my best."

All the other passengers were getting on board, but Harry knew Ray had one more person he needed to say goodbye to.

Eleanor.

She stood there, looking forlorn and miserable—but when Ray set his gaze upon her, she wiped her eyes and offered him a brilliant smile.

Ray pulled her into his arms and, with all the onlookers gawking, he kissed her, right there on the platform.

His sister giggled, his mother scolded, and his father smiled.

Harry noticed that Mabel looked away and Eileen looked down. He'd often wondered if they'd secretly been pining after Ray.

The train started to chug, slowly picking up steam as it made its way out of the station.

Ray was forced to let Eleanor go, and when he did, he said, "Promise me you'll be here when I get back?"

"I promise," she said.

He grinned and lifted his bag over his shoulder to catch the train. After jumping on, he tossed his bag *inside and, holding the rail with one hand, he hung off the side and waved with the other.*

*Everyone on the platform waved to him, calling out, cheering for him and wishing him well.*

*Eleanor waved her handkerchief over her head. She was the last person waving as the train disappeared down the tracks.*

*People started to leave the platform until it was just Eleanor, Mabel, and Harry standing there, lost in their own thoughts.*

*When Eleanor turned back to the depot, Mabel stepped into her way. For a long time, the two women stared at each other. Harry frowned, surprised at their animosity toward one another.*

*"Remember what I said," Mabel said to Eleanor.*

*Eleanor lifted her chin and wiped her tears as she moved around Mabel and disappeared into the depot.*

*Mabel's shoulders fell, and she lowered her face into her hands and hurried off the platform.*

*Harry just stood there, confused and befuddled.*

*It seemed strange to go back to life as normal after Ray was gone, but Harry had little choice. There was a job to do, and he'd promised Ray he would do it well.*

*Eleanor looked so miserable, Harry didn't want to bother her with his idea, at least not yet. He'd give her time to mourn Ray's departure, and then he'd bring it up.*

*There was a pall over the depot those first few days following Ray's absence. Harry had always known that Ray was an important member of the depot, but until he was gone, he hadn't known how much the affable young man had meant to so many people. Each new group of volunteers who came in to take on a shift would ask if Ray had gotten off all right, and then the mourning would start all over again.*

*But it was hardest on Eleanor. She had told Eileen that she didn't plan to sing that week for the canteen dance—not with Ray gone. And he sure couldn't blame her. Someone else would need to be found to play an instrument, or they might not be able to hold the dance.*

*One woman said she knew how to play the piano and volunteered, but it wouldn't be the same.*

*On Wednesday, five days after Ray left, Harry decided it was time to approach Eleanor about his idea. He was convinced it was the perfect plan.*

*He had just finished getting some passengers settled in the waiting room and putting their luggage on the storage wagon when he saw Eleanor walking toward the depot with a brown paper package in her hand. The bloom had gone out of her cheeks, and Harry hadn't seen her smile since Ray left.*

A new crew of volunteers was coming on duty, and the depot bustled with activity. The next troop train was due at any moment, and the ladies scrambled to be ready.

Once Eleanor got into the depot, she'd be put to work making sandwiches, and Harry wouldn't get a chance to talk to her again until later. And there might be others around to hear.

What he had to say, he wanted to tell her without an audience.

He left the depot and crossed the road to meet Eleanor on her way.

She looked up, clearly surprised to see Harry standing there.

"Hello," he said with a smile.

"Hi, Harry." She didn't return the smile, but she stopped. The thin parcel in her hands looked to be the same size as the record she'd given Ray. "Is there something I can do for you?" she asked.

Harry took off his stiff porter's hat and clutched it to his chest, suddenly nervous about his idea. He wanted to help Eleanor and Ray, but maybe they didn't want his help.

"Don't be shy," Eleanor said, her eyes softening, coming close to a smile though it didn't quite materialize.

"I'm really sorry Ray left," Harry said. "He's like a brother to me, and I'm going to miss him."

"He spoke fondly of you. I'm sure he'll miss you too."

"Well." Harry cleared his throat. "I had an idea. It came last Friday night when you gave Ray that record, do you remember?"

"Of course I remember." She frowned, looking truly curious. "What kind of an idea did you have?"

He clutched his hat hard and took a deep breath. "There were two men on the passenger train that came through that night, and I overheard them talking. They both liked your singing and said you had a great career ahead of you. One of them said that if he had time, he would stay in Dennison to try to convince you to go to New York City to audition for a record company."

Eleanor lifted her eyebrows and blinked a couple of times, as if she was trying to absorb what he had just said.

"They sounded serious," Harry continued. "They truly thought you have a gift and you could make it as a professional singer in New York City."

"Me?" Eleanor swallowed, looking down at her package. "I—I always hoped and dreamed, but I didn't think I could actually do something like that."

"They sure think you can." Harry started to get excited again. "And I think so too. All you need to do is buy a train ticket to New York City so you can audition for those men. By the time Ray comes home, you'll be a star and making so much money, you and he can get married and make a life for yourselves right off."

"I don't know if I have it in me to go off to New York all by myself, without a guarantee that I'll get a record contract." She shook her head, frowning again.

He was afraid she'd say that—and he was ready with another suggestion. "Then make a record, like you did for Ray, and send it in to the record company. Once they hear your voice, I know they'll want you to go to New York to show them more. Maybe they'll even pay for you to go there."

Eleanor pressed her lips together, and Harry could see that she didn't like the idea. She readjusted the parcel in her hands.

"I don't know," she said, starting to walk toward the depot again. "I don't think it's a good idea, Harry. I appreciate your help, but I think I'll just stay in Dennison until Ray gets back, and then we'll move to New York and try it together. I don't want to go there by myself."

Harry's disappointment was so intense that he had to look away from Eleanor for a moment, not wanting her to know how much hope he'd already put into this plan. He wanted Eleanor to succeed for her and *Ray's* benefit.

He followed Eleanor toward the depot, not willing to give up so easily. There had to be a way to convince her.

"What's the worst thing that could happen? If you send off the record and they want to hear more, I'm sure one of the other gals would go with you to New York. You wouldn't have to go alone."

She still didn't look convinced and kept walking.

He was desperate to get her to stop. "What do you have there?" he asked, nodding at the parcel, hoping it was a record of her voice.

"I'm sending this off to my teacher in New Philadelphia. It's a record, like the one I gave to Ray. Miss Canterbury is the only other person who believed in my dream, so I wanted her to have one too."

Excitement surged through Harry. "That's perfect! Why don't you send it off to a record company instead? All you have to do is change the address. Just think of the possibilities!"

"I can't do that, Harry. I only had two records made, and I can't afford another. This one is for Miss Canterbury."

"But if you become famous, you can send her all kinds of records, right?"

Eleanor frowned. "I don't know, Harry. What if they laugh at it?"

"Laugh? They'll be happy you sent it. I know it."

She bit her lip. "Maybe."

It was all Harry needed to hear. "Don't hesitate. Go on and do it before you change your mind. You won't need to do this alone. We're all here for you."

Hope lit up her eyes, and she gave a slight nod.

A train whistle blew in the distance, and Harry knew he'd need to hurry to meet it on the platform. "Go on," he prodded Eleanor. "You'll see I'm right."

Without another word, Eleanor left, carrying her record toward the post office in the depot.

Someday, Ray would thank Harry for prodding Eleanor one step closer to her dream.

"And so," Harry said to Debbie as he finished telling her the story, "I was the one responsible for Eleanor's disappearance."

"How?" Debbie asked. "You suggested she send a record to a company in New York. What makes you think it was your fault that she left and didn't tell Ray where she went?"

Harry studied Debbie for a moment. "I know," he said quietly, "because the day before she left, several months after I encouraged her to send the record off to New York, she got a real important-looking letter in the mail. I only had a chance to glance at it, so I didn't see where it was from, but the way she acted, all nervous and uncertain, told me it was significant. And then, the very next day, she left town without saying a word to any of us."

"And she never came back," Debbie finished for him. "So you think she got an offer from a record company?"

"That's what I've always thought."

"But you never heard about her again, right? You didn't hear that she became a famous singer, did you?"

"No," Harry said slowly, "but that doesn't mean she didn't go to New York to try. Maybe she got there and it didn't work out, but something else came up, setting into motion a series of events that caused her to abandon Ray. And if that's the case, then it's my fault."

A soft breeze ruffled Debbie's hair as she listened to Harry.

Crosby nudged her hand, reminding her that he was there and he needed to be petted. "Why didn't you ever tell Ray any of this?"

Harry looked down at his lap, his shoulders slumped. "I was too upset about it. I kept hoping he'd find her. He went to New York looking for her, so I assumed if she was there, he'd bring her home.

He didn't. After he came back, I didn't think it much mattered anymore what I had done."

Debbie thought about everything Harry had said, but it didn't add up with what she knew about Eleanor. The girl had been young and inexperienced. It didn't seem likely that she'd go off to New York all by herself.

But, then again, maybe she had—and maybe Harry's well-intentioned interference *had* caused her to leave Ray. She needed more information.

It was time to talk to Ray again and see what he'd discovered when he went to New York looking for Eleanor.

# CHAPTER EIGHT

*D*ebbie hoped to visit Ray on Thursday morning, but nothing seemed to go as planned from the moment she woke up.

The sky was overcast, and the clouds were thick with the threat of rain. Debbie had overslept and had to rush to get ready, knowing Greg was coming that morning with the electrical inspector. Once the wiring was approved, Greg would hang the drywall so the taper could come and prepare the rooms for painting.

As Debbie got ready, she tried to analyze why she felt the need to take extra care with her appearance today. She usually didn't wear much makeup, especially since leaving her job in Cleveland, where she had dressed in business-casual every day. Most of her work clothing was shoved to the back of her closet, and she didn't expect to have any reason to don a business suit or high heels anytime soon.

Yet she put on some mascara and touched up her hair with a curling iron. She wanted to look nice for Greg—there, she'd admitted it to herself. She knew it was silly. Not only was she starting a new chapter of her life, one that required all of her attention and focus, but Greg was a single dad with two teenage boys, and there wasn't much time in either of their lives for dating.

At least, that was what she kept telling herself. It was one thing to be interested in a man—another to think about dating him.

Besides, Greg had shown no particular interest in anything other than friendship.

But that didn't mean she couldn't put a little extra time into her appearance when she knew she'd see him.

The front doorbell rang, and Debbie quickly unplugged the curling iron, checked one last time in the mirror to make sure she looked presentable, and then ran down the stairs to the front door.

Greg stood on the stoop, his ready smile in place, though there was something different about it today. As if he had bad news. She looked down and then over his shoulder. She could see Hammer's head hanging out the truck window. That couldn't be a good sign.

"Good morning," Debbie said, trying not to sound breathless from her sprint.

"Good morning." His eyes crinkled at the edges when he smiled and took her in. "You look nice. Going somewhere special today?"

Heat warmed her cheeks as she looked down at her shorts and blouse, trying not to be obvious that she'd taken pains with her appearance for him. "Thanks. I hope to run over to Good Shepherd today to see Ray."

"I'm sure he'll notice how pretty you look too." As soon as Greg finished his sentence, he seemed to realize how forward it came across, and pink tinged the tips of his ears.

Debbie smiled to herself and motioned for him to come inside then closed the door behind him.

"How's the investigation into Eleanor's disappearance going?" Greg asked.

"Well..." Debbie turned back to face him, relieved that he had changed the subject, although she wasn't sure how to answer the question. "I'm learning a lot more about the situation, but I don't think I'm anywhere close to figuring out what happened. I know there are two individuals who think they had something to do with her leaving Dennison, but it's only speculation, no proof. One thinks she scared Eleanor away, and the other thinks he was responsible for getting Eleanor a big musical break. That's why I'm hoping to talk to Ray and see what he knows about those theories."

"Even if they aren't responsible, maybe their stories will spark a different idea or possibility in Ray's mind. I'm sure he'll take anything."

"I hope you're right," Debbie said. "And each clue seems to be leading me to the next, so that's been helpful. I'm kind of stuck right now though, so I was hoping Ray could shed some light."

"Speaking of light." Greg gave her a tight smile. "I have all the electrical run in the basement, and I was supposed to meet the inspector here this morning, but he just texted and said something came up and he can't get here until later today. I was planning to get the drywall hung right after his inspection, because I have the taper coming early tomorrow morning. I don't want to have to reschedule with him, because he agreed to squeeze your job into his busy schedule and if we have to postpone, he might not be available before your friends get here."

Debbie tried not to let her disappointment show, but she didn't think she was doing a very good job.

"But," Greg said quickly, "I can work late tonight, so if you don't mind me being here, I can probably come back later with the boys and we can get it done."

"You'd do that for me?" Debbie asked, a little surprised. "Work late, I mean?"

"Of course." Greg smiled. "I know how important it is for you to get the basement rooms done by the time your friends come, so I'll do whatever it takes."

"That's really sweet. Thank you."

"I learned a long time ago that my job requires patience and flexibility. Things rarely go as planned, so we have to adjust and make the best of it." He chuckled. "Not unlike life in general."

"That's true." Very few things had gone as planned in Debbie's life. "I never expected to be living back in Dennison or opening a café. But look at me now."

"Sometimes the best experiences in life come out of the unexpected." His gaze rested on her face for a moment, and then he cleared his throat. "I'll shoot you a text when the inspector lets me know his arrival time, and we can work from there. Does that sound good?"

"Sounds great. And, if you and the boys are here for supper, I can order some pizzas or make a big batch of spaghetti."

"Pizza is always welcome. The boys love it."

"Okay, pizza it is."

"I don't have much else I can do until the inspector takes a look at the electrical, so I'll head over to the house I'm flipping right now and check on how my crew is doing. I'll see you later."

"Definitely. I'm planning to stop at the café to see if the chairs have been delivered yet, and then I'm heading over to visit with Ray. I should be home by midafternoon."

"Great. Tell him hi for me." Greg left the house, leaving the subtle scent of his cologne in his wake.

Debbie closed the door behind him, realizing that her heart beat a little faster and wishing she wasn't so disappointed in knowing that he wasn't going to be around the house that morning.

But it was almost better to look forward to seeing him later. She enjoyed Jaxon and Julian—though they had said very little to her—and she hoped to get to know them better too.

Maybe some of life's best experiences really *did* come out of the unexpected.

Greg Connor was definitely unexpected.

"Are you sure you don't want to call the upholstery guy again?" Janet asked Debbie a couple of hours later as they drove out to the assisted-living home.

"What's the point?" Debbie asked, blowing a strand of hair out of her eyes with a frustrated puff. "You called already, didn't you?"

"Yes, but if you call too, maybe they'll take us seriously."

"Or maybe they'll get frustrated and stall the process even more." Debbie turned onto the drive leading up to the home and shook her head. "What if we don't get the chairs in time for the grand opening? It's just over two weeks away. They said we'd have them by now."

"I know." Janet let out a sigh. "The guy I spoke to said there's been a holdup, and he promised we'd have them by the grand opening. But that's not my biggest concern right now. Dale didn't show up at all today, and he still hasn't started on the restroom."

Debbie gripped the steering wheel, trying not to let her frustration boil over. "Do you think we should hire someone else?"

"Who? Everyone's busy. We might be able to get someone who's willing to do us a favor, but even that isn't guaranteed."

"I would suggest asking Greg Connor, but he's working on my basement and has his hands full with other projects."

"I don't want to take him away from your basement," Janet said. "I know how much you want to get your project done before Danica and Cori get here. I wouldn't ask you to give that up. There has to be a different solution."

"I could ask my dad," Debbie offered tentatively. "He's been itching to do something, and he has experience with projects he's done on his house."

"Does he know how to run plumbing?"

"No, but he can paint and lay tile. Maybe we need to take over the contractor's job and line up subcontractors to do the work. I can see if Greg knows of a plumber who might be willing to come in. The wiring is already in place, so we would just need someone to attach the light fixtures. I know my dad has done that in the past. And then he could do the rest of it."

Janet nibbled her bottom lip. "I'll call Dale this afternoon and tell him that if he can't get the restroom started tomorrow, we're going to look for someone else."

"Deal." Debbie pulled into the parking spot at the home.

Large raindrops began to fall as they stepped out of the car. Debbie glanced up at the sky as more and more raindrops plummeted to the earth. She opened the back door and reached for the small trunk with the old newspapers they'd found in the attic. She had promised Ray that she'd bring them to him.

It was heavy, but Janet came around to close the door for Debbie, and then they rushed into the large building.

They were both laughing as they entered and almost didn't see the woman who was just leaving.

"Oh, I'm sorry," Debbie said as she stepped out of the woman's way, the trunk awkward in her arms. Then she noticed that it was Susan Donlea, and smiled. "Hello."

"Hi." Susan nodded at both of them and looked outside. "It appears I've chosen a bad time to leave."

"It looks like it might be raining for a little while," Janet agreed.

"I have you two to thank for cleaning out my attic," Susan said. "After I spoke to you the other day, I started missing my mother, so I went through some of her things. I think I might donate a few items from her canteen days to the depot museum. I was just here dropping off a few things that I thought Eileen might like."

"How nice," Debbie said, trying not to wince at the weight of the trunk.

Susan looked outside and shook her head. "I might as well brave this storm now. It doesn't look like it's letting up anytime soon, and I'm babysitting my granddaughters this afternoon. I should get going."

"Have fun with your granddaughters," Debbie said. "We look forward to seeing you again soon."

Susan waved goodbye and left the building. Janet turned to Debbie. "Do you want me to hold the trunk for a while?"

"I've got it," Debbie assured her as they walked up to the counter to inquire where they could find Ray. After learning that he was probably in his room, they got the number and headed in that direction.

Ray sat near his window, his Bible in hand, dozing, when they knocked on his open door.

"Hello?" Debbie said. "Ray, are you up for some visitors?"

Ray looked up quickly and blinked a couple of times before smiling. "Come in, come in," he said. "It's not every day that I get two pretty ladies at my door."

"Ray, this is my friend and business partner, Janet Shaw."

"It's nice to meet you, Ms. Shaw." Ray offered his hand for her to shake.

"The pleasure is all mine, Mr. Zink. But please, call me Janet."

"Okay. And you can call me Ray," he said as he motioned to a couple of chairs. "Have a seat." He frowned. "What do you have there?"

"It's the trunk of newspapers from your attic," Debbie said as she looked for a place to set it down.

His eyes lit up. "What a treat it will be to relive the old days through those newspapers. Thanks for bringing them by."

Debbie set the trunk on the floor and noticed that Eleanor's record was on his nightstand. "Have you had a chance to listen to that yet?"

Ray's eyes were bright as he wheeled himself over to Debbie. "I've been listening to it almost constantly since you brought it to me. Would you like to hear it?"

Debbie and Janet had heard the record the day they'd found it, but Debbie knew Ray would like to play it for them, so she nodded.

"I would love to hear Eleanor sing." She took the record out of its sheath and gently set it on the turntable of the phonograph that Ray had set up on his dresser. When the record was spinning, she slowly set the needle on it.

The sound of Eleanor's voice filled the room. As the record played, Ray's face transformed into that of a man deeply in love. Tears filled his eyes, and he let them fall unashamedly.

"That's my Eleanor," he said quietly. "My sweet, beautiful Eleanor. Sounds just like she did at the canteen dances."

When the song came to an end, Janet handed Ray a tissue, and he wiped his wrinkled cheeks. "I never thought I'd get to hear her again before you brought this back to me. Thank you so much for this gift."

Debbie almost didn't want to bring up Mabel's or Harry's claims, but she desperately wanted to help him find his lost love.

"I came here today to tell you what I've learned," she said. "And ask if you've thought of anything else that might be helpful."

Ray finished wiping his cheeks and then pushed himself over to the chairs near the window.

He clutched the tissue in his hand. "What have you learned?"

Debbie took a deep breath. "I spoke to Mabel Holman's daughter, Susan, and she told me that Mabel was in love with you before you left for the war."

Ray frowned, his eyebrows dipping deep. "She was what?"

"Susan claims that Mabel was in love with you and planned to tell you right before Eleanor arrived, but she didn't get a chance. Apparently, right before you left Dennison, Mabel approached Eleanor and told her to let you go. She believed that her warning was what prompted Eleanor to leave Dennison."

"What? Why would she do such a thing?" Ray looked like he could come out of his chair any second. "And why didn't she tell me? Mabel was here when I got back. She saw how desperate I was, but she never said a word." He frowned. "If I remember correctly, she married Sam Holman soon after I returned to town. They met at the canteen when his troop train came through Dennison and wrote to each other all throughout the war. After they got married, they bought a farm outside of town. She had years to tell me what she had done."

"Do you really think her one conversation with Eleanor is the thing that made her leave?" Janet asked softly.

Ray sighed and shook his head, melting back into his chair. "It probably wasn't."

"But that's not all," Debbie said. "I also spoke to Harry Franklin."

Ray's grin brightened his face. "Harry's a lifelong friend."

"It seems he thinks he's responsible for Eleanor's disappearance too." Debbie watched Ray's lips turn from a smile to a frown again.

"How's that?" he asked.

"Apparently, he encouraged Eleanor to send one of her records to a record company in New York City. Several months later, when she got an official-looking letter in the mail, she left the very next day. He thinks it was an offer to go to New York."

"What?" Ray looked truly perplexed. "That can't be true. Harry would have told me."

"He was upset," Debbie said. "And he said that you went to New York but didn't find Eleanor, so he didn't think it mattered anymore."

Ray's shoulders fell, and he nodded. "If she'd been in New York City, I think I would have found her. I searched in every possible place I could think of, inquiring after her for weeks. No one ever heard of her—unless she changed her name." He let out a weary breath. "I guess I don't blame Harry for not saying anything. I probably would have been pretty upset about it too if I were him. He didn't mean anything by it." Ray looked up at Debbie and searched her gaze. "But do you think Eleanor went off to pursue a record deal and then got so famous that she didn't want to associate with me anymore? I never heard of her becoming famous, but she could have changed her name."

"I don't know. I still need more clues." Debbie nibbled her bottom lip. "I'm hoping you might have remembered something you could tell me."

Ray looked at Debbie for several moments, but then he shook his head. "I've been looking for Eleanor O'Reilly for seventy-eight years. If I knew anything else that might be helpful, I would have thought of it by now."

Debbie nodded. "I understand."

"If you do think of something," Janet said, "be sure to tell us."

"You're helping too?" Ray asked with a smile.

"Of course." Janet returned his grin. "Debbie and I are a team now, and the depot is like another home. Anyone who ever worked there is family, and family sticks together."

"I like this one," Ray said to Debbie with a laugh.

Debbie smiled at Janet.

Hopefully something more would reveal itself soon. Maybe the very next clue would be the key to unlocking the mystery.

## CHAPTER NINE

It was still raining when Debbie dropped Janet off at her car near the café. Greg had texted her and said he was at her house with the electrical inspector, so she had told him where she hid the spare key. His boys were with him, and he hoped that they could start working on the drywall as soon as the inspector gave him the all clear.

Debbie couldn't help but be excited at the prospect of seeing Greg again. The more time she spent with him, the more she liked him. He was funny, intelligent, and hardworking. She wasn't surprised that he was the president of the chamber of commerce or that his business kept him so busy. No matter where she went in town, whenever she mentioned that Greg was working on her house, people always had the nicest things to say about him.

He made it easy to like him.

It didn't hurt that he was handsome and that his dimples gave him a charming quality that made her smile.

Debbie stopped at Pangrazio's Pizza, not too far from the depot, and ordered two large pizzas to go. It was her favorite restaurant as a kid growing up in Dennison.

"Hello, Debbie!" the clerk, Danny, according to his name tag, called when he saw her. He wore a white apron, stained with sauce. "I heard you were back in town."

"I came a few weeks ago," she replied with a smile. "I'm opening—"

"The Whistle Stop Café," Danny supplied for her. "We heard. And you bought Ray's old house. How are the renovations going? I heard Greg was working in the basement, finishing off some bedrooms for you."

Debbie chuckled to herself, trying not to be so surprised that everyone knew her business in town. It was a tight-knit community, which was one of the reasons she loved it so much. Some of her friends had been impatient to graduate high school and move to a big city where people didn't know so much about them, but that hadn't been why Debbie left Dennison. She'd left for college and stayed in Cleveland to be closer to Reed before he was deployed.

"The renovations are going well," Debbie said. "I'm actually here to order supper to take to Greg and his boys. They'll be working late tonight to get the drywall up in time for the taper, who comes in the morning."

"Very good," Danny said. "I can't wait to hear how things go."

Debbie wanted to say that she was sure he would hear but just smiled instead.

The pizzas smelled delicious as Debbie left the restaurant and returned to her car twenty minutes later. Her house wasn't far away, so they'd be piping hot when she got there.

It was still raining hard, causing her to drive slowly through town. When she arrived at her house, Greg's red truck was parked out front.

Her stomach did a strange flip, taking her by surprise. Greg would probably laugh to know that she had formed a little crush on him—because that was the only thing it could be. She was clearly attracted to him, though she tried hard not to be. She hardly knew him—and, more importantly, she wasn't ready to be dating. Not so soon after coming back to Dennison.

Besides, she wasn't sure she could ever love anyone the way she had loved Reed.

She pulled into her driveway, and the kitchen door opened. Julian, Greg's younger son, emerged with a grin on his face. He ran over to Debbie's car and stood there, waiting. She jumped out and would have been worried that something was wrong if it wasn't for his grin.

"Dad sent me to help you with the pizzas," Julian said over the noise of the rain.

"They're on the passenger seat," she said.

He opened the door and grabbed the pizza boxes while Debbie reached for the bottle of soda she'd also purchased—but Julian managed to grab that too.

"I can get it," she said.

Julian only grinned and headed back toward the house, balancing the pizza boxes in one hand and grasping the soda in the other.

Debbie closed the driver's side door and raced around the car to the house, where she opened the kitchen door for him.

"Thanks," he said.

The aroma of marinara sauce, pepperoni, and baked garlic crust wafted up to Debbie's nose as she held the door to let him pass.

Once inside, she heard the telltale sounds of construction coming from the basement. She heard the click of dog's nails on the basement steps, and a moment later Hammer skidded to a stop at her feet.

Her clothes were soaked and her hair hung around her face in wet clumps, but she took a moment to scratch behind his ears and tell him what a good dog he was.

"I'm going to run up and change really quick," she said when Hammer's nose led him to abandon her and eye the pizza boxes in Julian's hand. "Why don't you let your dad and brother know that the pizza is here?"

Julian set the boxes and soda on the counter out of Hammer's reach. "Okay," he said.

"I'll be right back." She raced upstairs and quickly changed into a pair of jeans and a dry T-shirt. One look in the mirror told her that her hair was a mess, but she didn't have time to do much with it. She didn't want to make the guys wait for her to start eating.

She quickly toweled off her hair and ran a brush through it then pulled it into a ponytail.

It would have to do.

As she walked down the stairs, she heard them talking. Greg's deep voice was mingled with the sound of his son's maturing voices.

She walked into the kitchen, and they all stopped talking and looked in her direction.

"Hey," Greg said with a smile. "The pizza smells delicious."

"Help yourself," she told them as she went to the cabinet and took out some glasses and plates. "There's plenty, and I'm planning to send you home with whatever you don't eat, so don't be shy."

The boys eagerly grabbed plates and filled them up with slices of the thick, gooey pizza.

"Don't start eating until Miss Debbie is at the table and we've prayed," Greg warned his boys.

"Yes, sir," they mumbled.

"We can eat in the dining room," Debbie told them. "The table is bigger in there."

The boys went into the dining room, and Hammer followed, an adoring, hopeful look in his eye.

"Thanks for the pizza," Greg said. "The boys are always hungry."

She smiled and took a couple of pieces then filled a glass with some ice and soda. "I've been meaning to get a pizza from Pangrazio's since coming back to town, but it's always nicer to eat with friends."

"We are friends, aren't we?" Greg asked, his voice a little quieter.

Debbie paused and looked up at him, her pulse ticking a bit faster. She nodded. "I think so."

"Good." Greg returned her smile.

They walked into the dining room where the boys waited. Jaxon was looking at his food, as if plotting the best course of action to devour the contents, but Julian watched Debbie—and then his father. His gaze slipped back and forth between them.

Debbie sat on one side of the square table, and Greg sat on the other. The boys were to her left and right.

No one spoke for a moment, and then Debbie asked Greg, "Would you like to say grace?"

"I'd be happy to." He reached for his sons' hands and they, in turn, reached for Debbie's.

She paused, not expecting them to hold her hands, but the simple act made her feel like part of this little family.

With a smile, she took their outstretched hands and then looked up to find Greg watching her. Something inscrutable passed over his features before he smiled and dropped his gaze, bowing his head.

Debbie wasn't sure what he was thinking—and she wanted to focus on his prayer.

After he finished, the boys dove into their pizza with gusto.

"You would think I raised them in a barn," Greg said as he shook his head and chuckled.

"Who can blame them?" Debbie asked. "This is good pizza. I loved it as a kid."

"So did I." Greg swallowed his bite. "I still can't believe we didn't know each other back then. How is that possible? We know all the same people."

"That's not hard in Dennison." She chuckled.

"Which is all the more reason it surprises me that our paths never crossed."

"Maybe we wouldn't have been friends, even if they had."

"That can't be true," Greg said with a smile. "I think I would have been very good friends with you, no matter when we met."

Debbie's cheeks filled with heat, and she noticed both Jaxon and Julian glance at her. Jaxon frowned, but Julian had more of a curious look on his face.

"Either way," Debbie said quickly, "I'm happy we finally did meet."

"So am I. Thankfully, it's never too late to make a new friend."

This time, the look Jaxon gave Debbie had daggers pointed right at her. It was clear he didn't like the way his dad talked to her, and though he seemed like a great kid, he wasn't pleased with the conversation.

She swallowed a bite, needing to change the subject.

"How's the drywall coming?" she asked.

It took a few seconds for Greg to adjust to the abrupt change in conversation, but he slowly nodded. "Good. We still have a lot of work to do. We might be here until late."

"I'm planning to help," she said. "Put me to work wherever I'm needed."

"I'll happily take your assistance," Greg said.

Jaxon continued to eat, but his scowl never left his face.

By the time they called it a night, Jaxon was in a full-blown mood. Greg had addressed his son's attitude several times, but instead of his mood improving, Jaxon seemed to get more and more upset.

"I'll be back in the morning with the taper," Greg said as he, Hammer, and the boys stood in the front entry with Debbie, getting ready to head home.

The rain had finally let up, so they would stay dry on their walk to the truck.

"Perfect," Debbie said. "I'll plan to see you then."

Jaxon ran down the porch steps, but Greg called out to him, "Be polite and say good night to Miss Debbie."

Pausing on the sidewalk, Jaxon stiffened, and then he turned. Through a tight mouth he said, "Good night."

"Good night, Jaxon."

"I'm sorry," Greg said. "I don't know what's gotten into him. He's usually a really easygoing kid."

Debbie knew exactly what was wrong with him. It didn't take a genius to know he didn't like the growing friendship between his dad and her—and she couldn't blame him.

"It's okay," she said.

"No." Greg shook his head. "I'll have a talk with him. No matter what, he doesn't have a right to be rude."

Debbie pressed her lips together, not willing to debate with Greg about how to raise his own child.

"Good night," Julian said with a quick nod of his head, holding the box of leftovers. "Thank you for the pizza."

"You're welcome."

Julian and Hammer took off, running down the sidewalk to catch up to Jaxon, who was getting into the cab of the truck.

Greg turned to Debbie. "I want to thank you too. I had fun tonight."

Debbie wanted to say she did too, but there was a part of her that knew she needed to put an end to whatever was developing between them. She had no desire to cause trouble with Greg and his sons—and that was exactly what had happened tonight. Debbie and Greg had flirted—just a little bit—but it was enough to make Jaxon angry. What might happen if they went on a date? Debbie couldn't be the person who came between a father and his son.

"I'll see you in the morning," she said as she took the doorknob in hand, a hint that she was waiting for him to leave.

He nodded. "Okay. Bye."

"Bye." She closed the door behind him and leaned against it for a moment, trying to catch her breath.

Tonight had been a good reminder to keep her focus on why she had come to Dennison—and it wasn't to fall head over heels for her contractor.

All week, Debbie thought about her evening with Greg and his boys. Whenever Greg was at her house to work, she tried to give him as much space as possible. Each time he'd say something flirtatious, or even close to flirtatious, she'd smile and try not to respond. She wasn't giving him the cold shoulder, just not encouraging him.

The truth was, she liked his attention and his playful nature, but every time she remembered Jaxon's scowl, she forced her thoughts to go in a different direction. She respected Greg and his sons too much to come between them.

To create more space between her and Greg, she spent a lot of time at the café with Janet that week. They were only nine days away from the grand opening, and there was still so much to do. Shipments of supplies had started to come in, and they spent much of the week organizing their storage room and refrigerator. Thankfully, Dale had taken them seriously about their restroom and was working steadily to get it done in time. And the upholsterer promised, once again, that the chairs would be ready before the grand opening.

As Debbie stood behind the counter in the café, taking inventory of their salt and pepper shakers that Thursday afternoon, her mind was going in a dozen different directions.

"I just emailed the corrected proof to the printers," Janet said as she came through the swinging door from the kitchen with her laptop in hand. She wore a pair of jeans and a T-shirt with a large cupcake in the center. Her apron also had cupcakes all over it. "Our menus should be delivered next Thursday."

"That's only two days before the grand opening," Debbie said as she set her clipboard on the counter. "Hopefully they're not delayed like everything else."

Janet shrugged. "If they are, we can always write the menu on the board along with our daily specials and muffins."

Behind the counter was a large chalkboard they had found at an antique store. After hanging it, Debbie's dad had made a new frame out of wide, white trim and tacked it in place. It was just where it needed to be for customers to see their daily specials and available baked goods, right when they walked into the café.

"It will all be fine," Janet said. "Everything is coming together, and we won't have anything to worry about."

"I like your optimism."

"How is your basement project coming along?" Janet asked.

"Great. The walls were all taped and mudded, and Greg sanded everything down before he painted them with a primer. He and the boys added the final layer of paint last night, and Greg hung the light fixtures I selected. He's working on the trim now. The carpet should be installed next Friday morning, bright and early."

"Isn't that the day that Danica and Cori are coming in?"

Debbie was a little nervous that the carpet layers couldn't come until the morning that her friends were due, but there was nothing she could do about it. With her parents' help, she should be ready for Danica and Cori's arrival. "They won't arrive until late afternoon, so there'll be plenty of time to move the furniture into each room after the carpet is laid."

"Will you need help hauling it in?"

"No." Debbie shook her head as she noticed Kim walking past the windows, outside the café. "My dad and mom are coming over in the afternoon to help. I'm sure you and I will be busy enough with the café that day. I wouldn't want to ask you to do more."

"Just let me know if I can be helpful. I'm sure Ian and Tiffany wouldn't mind helping either."

Kim entered the building, capturing their attention. She held a flat brown-paper package.

"Hi, Kim," Janet said after the little bell over the door chimed.

"Hi." Kim smiled at them and approached the counter, looking around the room with obvious approval. All the walls were decorated with framed WWII-era posters and antique kitchen appliances like an eggbeater, old cast-iron frying pans, and flour sifters that Janet had received from the baker who had taught her most everything she knew. "It looks amazing in here. Well done."

"Thanks." Debbie nodded toward Kim's hands. "What do you have there?"

"Oh!" Kim's face lit up with excitement. "I discovered something that I thought might be helpful." She set the thin package down on the counter. "A few years ago, we received a unique donation to the museum. It seems there was a bag of mail that had somehow been overlooked in the old depot post office for years, and when the postmaster figured it out, he thought it was too late to send the letters. He didn't want anyone to know he'd found it, so he brought it home and put it in his attic. Years later, after he had passed away and his family was cleaning out the attic, they found the bag and turned it over to the postal service. After a designated time, when no one claimed the mail, the post office donated it to the museum. I've looked through some of it before, but it's a big bag, and I haven't had a lot of time to catalog all the letters and packages to add to the museum collection."

Debbie's excitement started to mount when she saw Eleanor's name as the return address on the package.

It hadn't been opened.

"I got to thinking the other day about Eleanor," Kim said, "and since I knew the bag was from 1943, I figured I'd look through it and see if there was anything in there. Lo and behold, I did find something with her name on it!"

"May I?" Debbie asked as she reached for the package.

"Of course." Kim pushed it toward her.

"It's exactly the same size as the record I took to Ray," Debbie said as she pressed against the brown paper and felt the edges of a round disk under the cardboard sheath. "This has got to be the record that Harry thought Eleanor sent to a record company. She only had two made, and she gave one to Ray."

"Which means," Janet added, "that the record never made it to New York, so the official-looking letter that Eleanor received wasn't from a record company."

"And," Debbie said, "even if it had been sent, Eleanor didn't intend to send it to the record company. It's still addressed to Miss Celia Canterbury of New Philadelphia."

"It wasn't Harry's fault that Eleanor left town," Janet concluded.

"Does this help you?" Kim asked.

"Yes." Debbie nodded. "It at least crosses one possibility off the list."

"I bet Harry would like to see this," Janet said to Debbie. "It might ease his conscience."

"I saw him sitting out behind the depot right before I came over," Kim told them.

"I think I'll take it to him now." Debbie moved to the door. "Thank you, Kim."

"My pleasure. I'll keep looking to see if I can find anything else for you."

Debbie waved at her and left the café. Harry sat in his usual spot, Crosby at his side. A train was coming in from the west, and Harry watched it. But when he saw Debbie, he sat up straighter and tapped his hat to get it out of his eyesight.

Crosby's tail started wagging.

"Well, hello there, Miss Albright," Harry said with a big, welcoming smile.

"Hello, Mr. Franklin."

"What can I do for you today?" he asked.

Debbie presented the package. He reached for it, his eyebrows drawn together.

Slowly his expression changed from one of curiosity to one of complete and utter astonishment.

"Well, I'll be," he said with a shake of his head. "Where in the world did you find this?"

"Kim Smith had it in an old mailbag that was donated to the museum a few years ago. Apparently, the mail in the bag never left the depot post office, so the postmaster put it in his attic so no one would ever know. His family found it many years later, after he died, and the post office donated it to the museum."

Harry turned it over and saw that the seams were still sealed. "It never got sent to New York?"

"Never."

"So Eleanor didn't get an offer from a record company?"

"Not that I know of—and definitely not because you suggested she send it there."

The train passed by the depot, moving quickly. The rumble against the rails was loud and grinding, causing their conversation to halt. After several minutes, it was gone again.

"So I wasn't the reason she left Dennison?" Harry finally asked as he looked up at Debbie, hopeful.

"No." She shook her head. "You were not."

Tears gathered in his dark eyes, and he sniffled. "Well, shoot. I could have saved myself a lot of heartache if I had known that this record was never sent." He sighed. "I suppose I should visit with Ray and let him know what I did—unless you told him already."

"I did tell him."

He took a deep breath. "Is he mad at me?"

"I don't think so. He was upset for a moment, but a lot of time has passed, and I think he understood why you didn't tell him."

"I still owe him an apology though. I'll have to make a trip out to the Good Shepherd."

"I'm sure he would appreciate that." Debbie patted Crosby. The dog's tail started to wag again.

"Thank you for bringing this to me," Harry said as he handed it back to her. "What will happen to it now?"

Debbie held the package and looked down at it. "I'll return it to Kim, since it belongs to the museum. Maybe she'll put it on display."

"That would be nice. I like to think about Eleanor still singing in the depot lobby." He chuckled. "The men sure were in love with her, and after Ray left, it only got worse." Harry paused, his face revealing his surprise. "I just thought of something."

Debbie took the seat next to Harry, eager to hear what he had to say.

"There was a man." He pulled his thick eyebrows together as he searched the recesses of his mind. "Sam—or Steve—or Stan! Stan! That was his name. Stan Schroeder." Harry whistled. "That boy was head over heels in love with Eleanor, and he was at her side every waking moment after Ray left. At first, it seemed to bother Eleanor, but then she seemed to get used to it. Eventually, a lot of us were afraid she was falling for him. It wasn't right to steal another man's gal, especially when he was serving in the army." He paused. "Come to think of it, Eleanor left Dennison about the same time he did." Harry glanced up at Debbie, his eyes huge. "Do you think Eleanor eloped with Stan?"

Debbie leaned forward. "I don't know. Tell me everything you remember."

# CHAPTER TEN

*Everything about Dennison, Ohio, and the depot, irritated Stan Schroeder. The sight of ugly, black trains. The smell of grease and cinders. The sound of brakes and the grinding of the rails. But it was the troop trains he despised the most, because they reminded him, several times a day, that he wouldn't be going off to war to become a hero like all those other guys.*

*He scowled as he stacked flour barrels in the storage room, yet again. A local farmer had donated them earlier that day. The flour would be distributed to the volunteers who would use it to make bread, rolls, cookies, and doughnuts to give to the service members as they came through on the trains.*

*He had gotten away from his father's flour mill so he wouldn't have to see a flour barrel again—but here he was.*

*Though he hated working at the depot, he couldn't stay in his small hometown of Coshocton, not when he was so ashamed and embarrassed. When he'd heard that a job had opened in nearby Dennison at the depot, he'd jumped at the chance to come. But it wasn't any better here.*

*"Stan?" Eileen Palmer stepped into the storage room with a clipboard in hand. She wore her stationmaster uniform—a pencil skirt and blazer with a matching hat. She frowned at him. "Aren't you done with that yet? It didn't take Ray this long to unload four barrels of flour."*

Ray.

*Every time Stan turned around, he was being compared to the last guy who was the man-of-all-work at the station.*

*"I'm not Ray," he said under his breath.*

*"What?" Eileen had made it obvious that she wasn't a big fan of Stan since the moment he'd come to work at the station. Even though he was a year older than she and a foot taller. But, more importantly, he was a man. When he'd signed on to this job, he had no idea he'd be taking orders from a woman. If he didn't need the money and a reason not to return to Coshocton, he'd quit in a heartbeat.*

*"Nothing," Stan mumbled as he wiped his hands on his blue jeans.*

*Eileen stared at him, and he stared back, crossing his arms and planting his feet. He was a strong man, and he wasn't afraid to let her know she couldn't push him around.*

*But she didn't back down. Though she was small, she was tough. He would have respected her for it if he liked her, even a little.*

*"The canteen dance is tonight," she said.*

*"Yeah. There's one every Friday."*

*After pressing her lips together for a moment, she said, "I want you to set up the stage for Eleanor."*

*Just hearing Eleanor's name gave Stan a jolt. The first time he laid eyes on her, on his first day of work five months ago, he fell in love. But, of course, she was Ray's sweetheart, and no matter how hard Stan tried to get her to pay attention to him, she didn't even appear to notice he was alive.*

*"Please get the stage set up as soon as possible." Eileen turned and left the storage room without waiting for his reply.*

*Stan glared after her, but his gaze caught on Eleanor sweeping the depot platform. A cold wind blew, though they hadn't had any snow yet.*

*He left the storage room and jogged over to her, grabbed the handle of the broom, and took it away from her.*

She made a startled sound and turned, her pretty blue eyes wide. "What are you doing?"

"This is my job," he said with a slow, easy smile. "A pretty little thing like you shouldn't be making calluses on her hands with a broom."

"I'm not making calluses—I already have them," she said, tilting her head at him and putting her hands on her hips. "I've been sweeping floors since I was old enough to walk."

"Doesn't change the fact that you shouldn't have to." He leaned on the broom handle and admired her. She wore a pretty pink jacket with a matching hat on her head. Her blond hair curled on the ends and bounced on the breeze. "Has anyone ever told you that you look like Ginger Rogers?" The famous actress was one of his favorites.

"I do not look like Ginger Rogers." She held out her hand for him to give her back the broom. "Now, may I please keep sweeping?"

"Did you know you're the only bright spot in my day, Ellie?"

"I've asked you not to call me Ellie," she said, clearly trying to stay patient. "My name is Eleanor."

"Is Stan bothering you again, Miss Eleanor?" Harry suddenly appeared from inside the building. He always seemed to be around her.

Stan ignored him. "I wish you'd let me call you sweetheart, instead."

Eleanor lowered her gloved hand. "There's only one man who can call me that, and you are not him."

She turned and walked into the depot, leaving Stan to look after her. He chuckled to himself, knowing that eventually he'd wear her down.

Harry eyed Stan with a frown. "Miss Eleanor doesn't like when you talk to her that way. She's Ray's girl, and we don't take too kindly to men who try to steal soldiers' sweethearts while they're away."

Anger burned deep in Stan's gut. "I'd be a soldier too, if they'd let me."

Harry's face filled with curiosity. "Why wouldn't they let you enlist?"

Stan looked down at his hands and the skin along his wrists and forearms with revulsion. It was his own body that had turned against him, preventing him from going overseas to serve. "Ever since I was little, I've been allergic to wool. Wool!" He wanted to kick something or punch something, but he gripped the broom handle instead. "I get eczema wherever it touches me, and since the uniforms are made of wool, I'm disqualified to serve."

Empathy lined Harry's face. "I'm sorry you can't fight for your country. I know what it's like to be denied something just because you're born a certain way."

Stan usually assumed people took pity on him when they learned he couldn't enlist, but he knew Harry wasn't doing that. He was a good kid. A people pleaser, which irritated Stan on most days, but Harry really did care about everyone at the depot. And despite how Stan often treated him, he seemed to care about Stan too.

"Yeah, well, thanks," Stan said, trying not to let his emotions get the better of him. "I guess there's nothing we can do about it."

"There's always something we can do," Harry said, lifting his shoulders. "You might not be able to go to war, but you can help those guys who are going. I might not be able to run this station, but I can help Miss Eileen. Everyone is important."

Harry's eternal optimism rubbed Stan the wrong way. "You can tell yourself that what goes on here is important," he said as he looked at the broom. "But I'm not staying around for long. I aim to get what I want out of life."

And right now, I want Eleanor.

"I got work to do," Stan said, shoving the broom in Harry's direction. "See that the platform is swept."

Harry took the broom without complaining, and Stan left to set up the stage—and find Eleanor.

She was in the lobby setting out sandwiches for the next troop train. While all the other ladies from a *neighboring town gossiped and chatted like magpies, Eleanor worked quietly on her own.*

*No doubt she was thinking about Ray.*

*Stan stood for a second, wondering about Raymond Zink. From everything he'd heard, Stan was Ray's complete opposite. And it was clear that Eleanor was in love with Ray—so maybe he was playing this game all wrong. He'd been trying to set himself apart from Ray ever since he'd arrived, but maybe he needed to be more like Ray so Eleanor would pay attention to him.*

*Harry's warning came back to him. "We don't take too kindly to men who try to steal soldiers' sweethearts while they're away." But Stan wasn't too concerned. It wasn't his fault that he couldn't go to war. So why should Ray get to go to war and get Eleanor? Shouldn't Stan have at least one thing he wanted?*

*He wasn't one to apologize, since he was rarely wrong, but maybe he needed to apologize to Eleanor. Not that he figured she deserved it—but just in case she thought so.*

*Swallowing his pride, Stan walked over to the table where the sandwiches were being set out, and cleared his throat.*

*Eleanor paused and turned to look at him. Irritation glinted in her eyes, but she didn't say anything.*

*If this was going to work, it had to be believable. He quickly took off his hat, knowing his hair would be a mess, but he didn't much care. "I want to apologize, Eleanor. Ever since I got here, I've been trying to tell you I like you, but I haven't been doing a good job."*

*She blinked several times and truly looked surprised at his admission. "Th-that's okay, Stan."*

*It was working. Excitement built inside him, so he decided to give his apology a little more gas. "I hope you'll forgive me."*

*"Of course I will." She smiled, and his heart did a somersault. "There's no real harm done."*

*Several of the other ladies watched them, but he didn't mind. The more people who heard their conversation, the better. Maybe they'd tell Eleanor to give him a try.*

*"I hope you'll let me make it up to you," he said, clutching his hat.*

*"There's no need—"*

*"Do you have your own record player?"*

*She shook her head. "The only things I own are the clothes I wear. I came to Dennison with nothing else."*

*He hadn't realized until this moment that he didn't know much about her. He'd been eyeing her for months, teasing her, flirting with her, and trying to be noticed, but he had never stopped to get to know her. Why didn't she own anything? Where had she come from? Where did she want to go?*

*To his surprise, Stan wanted to know the answers to his questions.*

*"I have a record player and dozens of records," he said. "I'll let you borrow them, if you'd like."*

*"Really?" Her eyes lit up, as if she'd just been offered the greatest gift of her life.*

*"Sure. I can bring them by your house sometime."*

*She looked hesitant for a second, but then she nodded. "Okay." She told him where she lived, and he promised he'd drop them off for her.*

*As he walked away from the table to set up the stage, he felt a little lighter on his feet.*

*He had started to woo Eleanor O'Reilly, and, if he played it safe, he might be able to get her to forget about Raymond Zink once and for all.*

*A month had passed since Stan had apologized to Eleanor—and in that time, something strange had started to happen to him. At first, he'd been pretending—a lot. Pretending to be happy, pretending to like his job, pretending to get along with the people he worked with. But, slowly, as he faked his way into*

Eleanor's inner circle, he started to realize that his feelings about a lot of things were changing.

As he stood on the depot platform that last Tuesday afternoon in December, watching another troop train roll out of the depot with hundreds of men who left everything behind to fight for freedom, he wasn't as angry anymore. Sure, he was still sore about the whole thing, but his anger had dulled, and now he was just sad.

Maybe he'd been sad all along and it had come out as anger.

Stan didn't want to think too deeply about his feelings. He'd never been one to talk about them or even examine them. Life was complicated enough without worrying about how he felt.

The snowy platform was littered with wrappers from the sandwiches and baked goods the service members had devoured in the last twenty minutes. It was always this way after a troop train departed, since they had so little time to grab their food. Some waited to eat it on the trains, but others consumed it while standing there on the platform, dropping their wrappers in their haste to reboard. Coffee cups needed to be stacked and taken to the back of the station to wash, cigarette butts needed to be swept up and tossed out, and gum needed to be scraped from the floor so it wouldn't stick to anyone's shoes.

*It was a thankless job, and Stan would usually be bitter right about now, but Eleanor had started to change all that. She was so good and so kind, he couldn't help but see the world through her eyes once in a while.*

*After all the garbage was cleared away, the cups were in the sink where the volunteers would wash them, and the gum was taken care of, Stan entered the lobby with a dustpan full of cigarette butts and found Eleanor with her new friend, June Manley. The two of them roomed together at the Snodgrass house and had been inseparable since June came to Dennison two weeks ago. If Eleanor wasn't already the object of Stan's affection, June would have easily filled that spot. She was funny, vivacious, and always up for a laugh. Her bright red lipstick and painted red nails were just as vibrant as her personality.*

*But the most important thing about June was that in the two weeks since she'd come to town, Eleanor had started to laugh again.*

*They both looked up and saw Stan as they giggled and set out new magazines on a table. A Christmas tree still stood in one corner, and garland hung over the doors and windows. The canteen ladies had done a great job bringing holiday cheer to the depot, and the soldiers had appreciated it.*

But it was Eleanor's smile that drew Stan's attention. It made his heart pump harder as his chest filled with warmth.

"Good afternoon," she said to him, her laughter dying on her lips. "We just heard the last troop train was one of the biggest yet."

Stan dumped the contents of the dustpan into the garbage and set it aside.

Mabel Thomas entered the lobby and glanced in their direction. When Eleanor saw her, her back stiffened, and both women turned away from each other at the same time.

It was easy to see that the two of them didn't like each other, but Stan couldn't understand why. Mabel was one of the quietest gals who volunteered at the canteen, and Eleanor was the sweetest. Why wouldn't they get along?

Turning his attention away from Mabel, Stan leaned against the ticketing counter and said, "You gals look like you're having fun."

"Fun?" June asked in a saucy voice. "Dennison is about as fun as watching paint dry."

Harry wandered in, whistling a happy tune, and smiled at Eleanor. "Any letters lately, Miss Eleanor?"

"Letters?" she asked. "You mean from Ray?"

"Or whoever." Harry shrugged.

*"Who would send me letters, except for Ray?"*

*"I don't know." A twinkle lit up Harry's eyes.*

*June glanced at Harry with a frown. "Do you know something we don't?"*

*He shrugged again.*

*"Well," Eleanor said as she adjusted her apron over her pretty blue dress, "I did get a letter from Ray today." Her cheeks turned pink. "I almost brought it with me, just to keep it close."*

*June rolled her eyes. "Why are you wasting time on a fella who's not here, when there are literally hundreds of others who could show you a good time?"*

*Stan liked the way June thought.*

*Eleanor sighed, in a dreamy sort of way, and looked toward the corner of the room where she used to sing with Ray. "When you meet the right one, all the others become the wrong ones."*

*Stan hated Ray Zink. It was hard to compete with a man who wasn't standing in front of him—one that people seemed to idolize and put on a pedestal. He'd heard enough, so he decided he was going to do something about it. And, if he was lucky, he'd get June's support.*

*"How about marrying me?" Stan asked.*

*Eleanor, June, and Harry all turned to stare at Stan.*

*He hadn't meant to propose marriage, but it had slipped out—and the more he thought about it, the more he liked the idea. If Eleanor was his wife, he'd never have to compete with Ray or anyone else again.*

*"Marry you?" Eleanor asked, her eyes wide.*

*June glanced at Eleanor with astonishment, waiting for her answer.*

*Harry looked sick, as if he was going to lose his lunch right there in the depot.*

*"Sure," Stan said. "I could make you happy, Eleanor. Just give me a chance."*

*She didn't speak for a moment, and he was sure he had shocked her. Finally, she said, "I'm honored that you'd ask me, Stan. But I promised I'd wait for Ray, and that's what I intend to do."*

*Anger built up in Stan, but he forced himself to keep it hidden. "If you change your mind, I'll be here."*

*June grabbed Eleanor's hand and whisked her off, whispering energetically in her ear.*

*Harry stood there, his mouth hanging open.*

*"Eleanor's going to be my wife," Stan said. "You just wait and see."*

Debbie sat in silence as Harry conveyed the story to her, occasionally stopping as if trying to remember.

"Now, keep in mind I was only there for parts of it," Harry said to Debbie. "But it was only another week or so before Eleanor left Dennison, and a day after that Stan left too."

"After she got an official-looking letter in the mail," Debbie reminded him. "Correct?"

"Yes, ma'am," Harry said. "I saw the letter with my own eyes."

"Did the letter have anything to do with Stan?"

Harry scratched his head, knocking his hat out of place for a moment. He reset it before he answered. "Now, I don't rightly know. I'd forgotten all about Stan until this very moment. But it seems like a strange coincidence that he proposed and she left town around the same time he did. At the time, I was so convinced she'd gotten a letter from a record company, I didn't think she had left with Stan. But now I'm not so sure."

"Did you ever hear from him again?" Debbie needed to have more evidence to suggest that Eleanor ran away with Stan Schroeder. From Harry's account, his personality left much to be desired. He didn't seem like the kind of man who could charm Eleanor away from Ray. But could he have *taken* her away? Was he capable of abducting her?

That changed everything.

"I never did hear from Stan again," Harry said, "but someone mentioned that they saw him in Cleveland after the war." He frowned. "I think it was Cleveland. Either Cleveland or Columbus. One of the two."

"Cleveland or Columbus," Debbie repeated. "I'll start my search for him there. Maybe I can find out if he and Eleanor ended up getting married."

"I sure hope they didn't," Harry said. "I wasn't a big fan of Stan Schroeder. He had a chip on his shoulder if I ever did see one. Wasn't a lot that could make that man happy but Eleanor."

"Thank you for sharing your stories with me. They've been very helpful."

"You're welcome. Come see me whenever you'd like. Crosby and I will be waiting for you."

Debbie smiled and said goodbye, eager to see if she could locate Stan Schroeder and find out what happened to him—and possibly Eleanor.

# CHAPTER ELEVEN

The smell of pot roast wafted up to Debbie as she opened the oven door to check on the progress of supper. She'd invited her parents over, and they would be there in about fifteen minutes. Potatoes boiled on the stovetop, and Debbie had the butter and milk warming in a saucepan to make mashed potatoes as soon as they were done cooking. Janet had baked rolls at the café earlier, and those were warming next to the roast.

With a vase of fresh flowers on the dining room table, everything was set for Debbie's parents, giving her a few minutes to jump on her computer and see if she could locate a Stan Schroeder in Cleveland or Columbus.

She took a seat at the kitchen table and opened her laptop. She kept her eye on the potatoes to make sure they didn't boil over and watched the timer she'd set for the bread.

It was hard to know where to start her online search, so she simply typed Stan's name with Columbus, Ohio, in the search engine to see what would pop up. There were three Stan Schroeders, but they were all too young to be the one she was looking for.

Next, she put in the year 1943 and included Coshocton, Ohio, since she knew where he grew up.

Finally, she saw something that looked promising. An obituary from 1986 with a picture of a man in his sixties.

*COLUMBUS—Stanley R. Schroeder, 65, died Monday at his home of an apparent heart attack, according to a Franklin County Medical Examiner's spokesman.*

*He was born in Coshocton and graduated from Coshocton High School in 1940. After graduation he worked in his father's flour mill until leaving Coshocton in 1943 to work at the Dennison Railroad Depot. Shortly thereafter, he moved to Columbus and was employed by the Bell telephone company until his death.*

*Survivors include his parents, Herbert and Nina Schroeder, Coshocton; his two sisters, Jean Finstad, Coshocton; Mary Sukopp, Coshocton; and his daughter, Eleanor Pantzke, Columbus.*

The rest detailed when and where the service would be held. Debbie stared at the name of his daughter. Eleanor. It couldn't be a coincidence. Had he named his daughter after the woman he'd been in love with? Had Eleanor O'Reilly become his wife? And why hadn't the obituary listed a wife? It had listed survivors but didn't mention who had preceded him in death. Had he married Eleanor and she died before him?

Debbie had so many questions, but the potatoes had boiled long enough and the bread timer went off.

She jumped up from the table, silenced the timer, and opened the oven to remove the rolls. When they were in a basket, covered with a cloth, she turned off the burner and took the pan of potatoes to the sink, where she poured them into a colander.

"Hello, knock, knock," Debbie's mom said from the kitchen door as she opened it slowly. "Can we come in?"

"Yes," Debbie said. "Dad's just in time to mash the potatoes, his favorite job."

Debbie's parents entered the kitchen with smiles on their faces. They loved that Debbie was back in town, and she knew they tried hard to allow her space while still making her feel welcomed and wanted.

"We brought dessert," Mom said as she held up what looked like an apple pie.

"Thank you." Debbie returned the potatoes to the pot and poured the melted butter and milk over them. "You can set it on the counter. I have vanilla ice cream or whipped cream for later."

"Mmm." Dad sniffed the air. "Pot roast?"

"Your favorite." Debbie loved that she was back in Dennison to enjoy her parents' company more often. Since Dad was now retired, he was especially eager to be involved in her life. Her mom still worked part-time as a receptionist at Trinity Health Systems, and she was busy volunteering at their church.

Mom set the pie down on the counter. "What's this?"

Debbie turned to see what she was asking about and noticed her mom was pointing at the laptop.

"Who is Stan Schroeder?" Mom asked.

"Isn't he that guy who lives in Uhrichsville?" Dad asked. "I think he owns a painting company."

"That's Sam Schneider," Mom said. "Not Stan Schroeder."

"Oh." Dad grabbed the hand masher and started on the potatoes. "That's right. Wasn't he married to the gal who started that dancing company?"

"Who?" Mom asked.

"Sam Schneider."

Mom shrugged. "I don't know anyone who started a dancing company."

Debbie smiled to herself as she listened to her parents' banter. Finally, after they settled who was who, she said, "Do you want to know who Stan Schroeder was?"

"That's right," Mom said, pouring herself a glass of water. "You were going to tell me why you were looking at his obituary."

She quickly filled them in on how she'd found the old record and taken it to Ray and how he'd asked her to help him locate Eleanor O'Reilly. After explaining all the leads and clues she'd found, she told them how they led her to Stan.

"Do you think Stan could have abducted her?" Dad asked as he continued to mash the potatoes.

"I doubt it." Debbie shrugged. "But I find it strange that he left Dennison around the same time and named his daughter after her."

"And you think this is the right Stan Schroeder?" Mom asked, pointing at the computer.

"Definitely. He was born in Coshocton, the age fits, and he named his daughter Eleanor. That seems like too much of a coincidence for it not to be the right guy."

"What will you do with the information?" Dad asked.

"I don't know. I'd like to talk to someone who knew him and see if he was married."

"Why don't you see if his daughter"—Mom paused and looked at the computer screen—"Eleanor Pantzke is still alive? Maybe she knows something."

"You're right." Debbie walked over to the computer and typed *Eleanor Pantzke Columbus Ohio* into the search engine. "What are the odds that she's still alive and living in Columbus?"

The first result to pop up on the screen was a social media page for Eleanor Pantzke of Columbus, Ohio.

"Looks like pretty good odds," Mom said with a chuckle.

Debbie clicked on the link. The woman in the profile picture looked to be in her late seventies. She had a wide smile, and she sat on a swing in a garden with two children by her side.

"Should I try to message her?" Debbie asked.

"Why not?" Dad wiped his hands on a towel. "What do you have to lose?"

With a shrug, Debbie clicked on the Messenger tab and wrote a quick note.

*Hello, Eleanor. My name is Debbie Albright. I live in Dennison, Ohio, where I believe your father worked and lived in 1943. It is my understanding that he worked with a woman named Eleanor O'Reilly at the Dennison Depot Salvation Army Canteen. I'm looking for any information you might have on Eleanor O'Reilly and would appreciate if you could message me back or call me at the number listed. Thank you for your time and attention to my request.*

Debbie reread the message and said to her mom, "Should I send it?"

"Go for it. I'm curious as to what she'll have to say."

"Okay." Debbie clicked the button. "It's done. Hopefully she can help us." She closed her laptop and turned back to the aromas of the meal. "I think we should take the roast out of the oven and let it sit for a minute while I show you the progress on the basement."

"Sounds like a good plan to me," Dad said.

"I'm excited to see it," Mom added. "Is it coming along like you had hoped?"

Greg hadn't been at Debbie's house that day, but he was almost done with the trim work and said he would have no trouble finishing it before the carpet layers came. Everything else was done.

"It is. I think Danica and Cori will be happy with the space."

Debbie opened the oven and took out the large roasting pan with two pot holders.

"I know you want to prove something to your friends," Mom said, "but you really don't owe anyone an explanation about why you chose to come back to your hometown."

Debbie set the roasting pan on a cutting board and lifted the cover. "I know."

"Do you?" Dad asked, his eyes growing serious behind his glasses. "Dennison isn't perfect, but it's a fantastic place to live. Your mom and I have been here our whole lives. We might not have skyscrapers and a Starbucks on every corner, but we have everything we need. And we have more than that. We have a tight-knit community of people who would drop everything and help us out if we say the word."

"Neighbors who bring over casseroles when you're sick," Mom added. "Teachers who stay late to help a struggling student. Doctors who still make house calls to the elderly or those who can't travel. And church members who leave their house in the middle of the night to help with emergencies."

"You don't need a big city to have purpose in life." Dad smiled at her. "All you need is a community of people to serve alongside. That's what's important in the long run. Your friends will know that."

Debbie gave each of her parents a hug. "You know what's better than skyscrapers and Starbucks?" she asked. "The two of you."

Dad kissed her head, and Mom squeezed her so hard, Debbie grunted.

"Now let's go look at my basement," Debbie said, laughing. "Before we all start crying."

They laughed with her as they followed her down the steps and into the basement.

She was excited to show off Dennison to her friends. She hoped they could understand how, since coming back to her hometown, she'd started to feel a part of something important and meaningful.

Helping Ray find Eleanor was the first of many things she wanted to do to be part of her community.

By Sunday, Debbie was ready for a day of rest. She had spent all day Saturday at the café with Janet, organizing the pantries, since most of the nonperishable food had been purchased and delivered. Dale had worked in the restroom, but by the end of the day, nothing seemed different, and Debbie wasn't sure if he'd actually done anything. What he did tell them was that he needed a new drain for the sink and, since it was an old sink, he'd have to special-order it, which meant it might not get there before the grand opening in a week. But he promised he'd do everything possible, so they didn't have anything to worry about.

At least that was what he said.

Sunshine poured through the windows of the Dennison Community Church as Debbie sat on a pew with her parents. The stained glass, which depicted the story of Christ's death and resurrection, reminded her of the Sunday school lessons of her childhood. She'd grown up in this church, establishing the foundation that she had built the rest of her life upon, so it felt like coming home to return here.

Pastor Nick Winston gave the sermon with as much passion and wisdom as he had when she was younger, making her smile and think.

After the service ended, Debbie stood up to leave the pew, and then she noticed Greg sitting a few rows behind them.

Their gazes caught, and he smiled.

She returned his smile, surprised that she hadn't seen him there the last couple of weeks she'd attended church.

"Hello," she said as she walked to his pew where Jaxon and Julian stood behind him.

"Hey," he said.

Jaxon tapped Greg impatiently on the shoulder. "Can I get by? I want to see Carrie."

Greg moved aside as both of his sons filed past him. Jaxon barely glanced at Debbie, but Julian smiled and said hi.

"Carrie is Jaxon's best friend," Greg explained. "They've been close since they were in third grade, and it still seems to be going strong."

"Third grade?" Debbie asked. "Really?"

"Yep. They were in Sunday school together and decided they would be friends forever. Neither one has changed their mind since then. It's been six years." He lowered his voice to a whisper. "I secretly think something more will come of it eventually, but we'll see."

Debbie watched as Jaxon joined a teenage girl at the back of the church. The girl seemed genuinely happy to see him.

"It feels good to be here," Greg said. "We've been out of town the past two Sunday mornings."

That explained why she hadn't seen them.

"Hey, Greg," Debbie's dad said, shaking Greg's hand. "Ready to play golf on Wednesday? I hear my team is up against yours."

"I heard the same." Greg grinned at him. "You're going to have to bring your A game."

"I always do." Dad laughed. "Say, we were at Debbie's house the other night, and she showed us your work in the basement. Good job. I couldn't have done better myself."

"I appreciate that, Vance," Greg said, turning his smile toward Debbie. "It's been a fun project."

Debbie enjoyed Greg's warm gaze, but a glance in Jaxon's direction suggested he was talking about her to his friend. They both looked at her, and Jaxon had a frown on his face.

"I should be able to wrap up the trim work on Monday," Greg said to Debbie. "Then I'll be out of your hair until the carpet layers come on Friday."

It was hard to believe that Greg had gotten everything done in her basement in less than two weeks, yet the restroom at the café was still unfinished.

"Debbie?" A woman tapped her on the shoulder.

Debbie turned and saw Susan Donlea. "Hi," Debbie said. "I didn't know you attended church here."

"Whenever I can," Susan said. "Though it's not as often as I'd like, since my work keeps me busy on the weekends."

Janet and Ian stood across the room, and when Debbie waved, they walked toward her.

"I was hoping I'd run into you and Janet," Susan said as she pulled an envelope out of her purse.

Greg still stood there, but Debbie's father and mother had turned away to talk to another couple they knew.

Janet walked up to their small group and said hello to Susan. Ian greeted Greg, and the two men started to talk about a chamber of commerce issue, making it clear they knew each other.

"I brought a letter I found in my mother's things," Susan said, handing the envelope to Debbie. It was yellow with age, but the handwriting looked similar to the handwriting that was on the undelivered package that Kim had found, and it was addressed to Mabel Thomas. "I think you'll find it very helpful."

"Can I read it now?" Debbie asked.

Susan nodded.

Her heart pounded hard as she pulled out the yellowed paper. It was a single sheet, with writing on one side. Would this letter hold a clue that pointed them in the right direction? A clue that Ray had never known?

Debbie unfolded the paper. The letterhead was from the Salvation Army, National Capital Area Command, Washington, DC, and dated March 17, 1944.

"Eleanor wrote this letter a little over two months after she left Dennison," Debbie said, doing the math quickly in her head. "And it looks like she was at the headquarters of the Salvation Army in Washington, DC."

Janet looked over Debbie's shoulder to see the letter, but Debbie still read it out loud.

"'Dear Mabel, I know we haven't spoken since I left Dennison, and you're probably surprised to get this letter from me. I've tried writing it at least a dozen times, but I can never find the right words, and my tears have stained the ink until it's illegible.'"

Debbie paused, moved by Eleanor's words.

"'I've thought a lot about what you said to me the week before Ray left Dennison, and I've come to realize you were right. I was never good enough for Ray, and you were the first person to realize it. When I left Dennison with June Manley, I had every intention of telling Ray where I had gone—but now it's impossible. June is right. She says I can't be the wife Ray needs anymore. He can't know where I am, and he can't come looking for me. Since I know you'll keep my secret safe, I'll tell you I have gone to Washington, DC, as you can see from the letterhead. I'm working as a secretary at the Salvation Amy Command Center with June. It wasn't my intention to abandon Ray, but events outside of my control prevent me from fulfilling my promise to him.'"

"Does she say what happened? Why she can't fulfill her promise?" Janet asked, impatient.

"Let me finish," Debbie said. "'Since I can't return to Ray, I wanted to let you know that I'm leaving him in your care. I know how much you love him, and perhaps your love will help him forget me. That is my hope and prayer. You were right all along. I would break Ray's heart, though that is the last thing I ever wanted. Please love him for me. Sincerely, Eleanor O'Reilly.'"

"That's it?" Janet asked, taking the letter from Debbie's hands.

"That's it." Debbie shrugged.

"Why did she go to DC?" Janet asked. "And what happened that was out of her control, keeping her from Ray? And who is June, and why would she convince Eleanor she shouldn't go back to Ray?"

"June Manley was Eleanor's friend," Debbie said. "From what Harry told me, she was quite a firecracker and a flirt. She gave Eleanor a hard time for being dedicated to one man when there were hundreds of others to have fun with."

"Do you think she encouraged Eleanor to date other guys and she fell in love with someone else?" Janet asked. "Was that why she couldn't keep her promise to him?"

Debbie shrugged. "I don't know what prevented her from coming back to Ray, but at least we know where she went."

"But we don't know why, or what happened to her after that." Janet sighed in frustration. "We can't just leave it here. Ray needs to know *why* she didn't tell him where she went."

"I agree." Debbie crossed her arms and bit her bottom lip. "I wonder if Kim would know how we might find information about someone who worked for the Salvation Amy Command Center in DC."

"We could also ask her to look for information about June Manley," Janet said. "You never know what we might find."

"I'll talk to Kim tomorrow," Debbie said. "Susan, thank you. There's a lot we still don't know, but at least we have another clue to help us track down Eleanor."

"We're one step closer," Janet agreed.

Debbie took the letter back and folded it gently, slipping it into the envelope. She held it out to Susan, but Susan put up her hand to reject it.

"Keep it," she said. "Maybe Ray will want it."

"Thank you." Debbie slipped the letter into her purse. "This is really helpful."

"You're welcome." Susan smiled. "I hope it helps you find Eleanor. I'm sure it's what my mom would have wanted."

Debbie hoped so too.

# CHAPTER TWELVE

*June Manley sighed deeply as she tapped her red fingernails against the sticky counter. The depot was quiet and lifeless after a large troop train had pulled out about twenty minutes ago. It was so cold, no one seemed to have energy. Even the volunteers from Uhrichsville who had come in at six that morning were quieter than usual. There was no laughter, no lighthearted teasing, no fun as they made hundreds of sandwiches in the prep room. Not even the promise of a New Year's Eve party that evening brought excitement to the depot. And if there was one reason June had left her boring hometown of Strasburg, Ohio, to come to Dennison, it was for fun. She hated that there was a war going on, but why not make the most of it and meet as many servicemen as possible? And where* better than Dennison, where they literally poured into the depot every few hours?

She'd left Strasburg the first chance she got, and for the first two weeks, she had a good time. But now? She sighed again.

Now, she was bored.

"You know what we should do?" June asked Eleanor, her roommate and best friend since arriving in Dennison.

"What?" Eleanor asked as she wiped down the counter June leaned against, forcing June to stand up straight.

"We should go to Washington, DC."

"Why?" Eleanor stopped wiping. She seemed to be the only person with any sort of enthusiasm today, but that was because she'd received another letter from Ray that morning. "Why would we do that?"

"It's where all the boys are," June explained, surprised she even had to. "A lot of military men are stationed there—we'd have more than twenty minutes of their time. Besides, it's where the excitement is right now. Washington, DC is at the center of the war effort— so what better place to go? Just think of all the exciting things happening there. I have a friend who lives near the Potomac River, right outside of Washington, in Alexandria, and she said the place is hopping. So many people are in the city, there's a housing shortage."

"Then why would we go there?" Eleanor asked. "Where would we live?"

"With my friend, silly. She grew up there, and we've been pen pals most of our lives. I met her through a school program where big-city kids were paired up with small-town kids to learn about each other's lives." June waved aside the explanation because it didn't really matter how she'd met her friend. "Shannon said that the Salvation Army is looking for girls to come to the command center to work, and since we already volunteer for the Salvation Army here, it would give us a better shot at getting a job there."

Eleanor frowned as she picked up some garbage from the floor and tossed it into a trash can. "I don't know, June. I wasn't planning to leave Dennison."

"Why not?" June threw her hands into the air and motioned to the empty lobby. "What in the world would keep you in Dennison? You don't have family here. You're as free as a bird. You can go anywhere you want. Why would you stay?"

"I like Dennison, and this is where I feel closest to Ray."

"Ray is overseas. You can always come back to Dennison when he does. But until then, you won't be any closer to him by staying here." June left the counter and put her hand on Eleanor's forearm. "Come with *me to Washington," she said. "I don't want to go alone. Just think how much fun we'll have there."*

*Mabel Thomas entered the lobby and cast her sullen expression toward Eleanor, causing June to want to stick her tongue out at her. Eleanor had never told June why Mabel hated her so much, but June had a few ideas. She wasn't sure how anyone could dislike Eleanor—unless Mabel was sweet on Ray. Eleanor had been like a sister to June since she arrived in Dennison to board with the Snodgrass family, and so any enemy of Eleanor's was an enemy of hers.*

*As Mabel passed through the lobby and disappeared into the dish room, June shook her head.*

*"It's not like you have anyone here who you would miss," she said.*

*"There's Ray's family. They've been kind to me."*

*"Have they invited you over for supper? Taken you in like a daughter?"*

*"No," Eleanor said slowly. "They don't even know that Ray proposed to me, so why would they?"*

*"Then why would you stay for them? You don't owe anything to anyone."*

*"Help me hang the New Year banner," Eleanor said, linking arms with June and pulling her over to the table where the decorations were. Someone had*

*just dropped off a huge crate full of them, and they needed to be set out around the room.*

*"Will the pleasures of this job never end?" June said in a dry, sarcastic tone.*

*Eleanor giggled and shook her head. "I'm afraid you'll never be content with an attitude like that."*

*"Who wants to be content?" June picked up a noise-maker horn and blew it. "Why be content when you can spend the rest of your life chasing adventures and romance?" She smiled. "You know how you feel about Ray? That's how I feel about every handsome man I meet."*

*Eleanor laughed even harder, and June couldn't help but laugh too.*

*Stan Schroeder entered the lobby from the platform door, a broom in one hand and a dustpan in the other. June had only known him for two weeks, but in that time, she had pegged him as a hothead, though he tried to be good around Eleanor. It was obvious that the man was besotted with her friend, especially after he'd asked her again yesterday to marry him. It was obvious that Eleanor was a little afraid of him. Whenever he volunteered to walk her home or stopped by the Snodgrass house to pay a call, Eleanor dragged June along to act as a buffer. June was afraid Stan was one match away from lighting his short fuse, and she didn't want to be around him if he exploded.*

*"Have you thought about my offer?" Stan asked, his gaze locked on Eleanor.*

*Harry appeared just then. He had an uncanny ability to be present whenever Stan approached Eleanor. June suspected it was out of protection for Eleanor and loyalty to Ray. He was one of the kindest boys June had ever met. The complete opposite of Stan.*

*"Don't be bothering Miss Eleanor with your silly proposals," Harry said to Stan. "She's marrying Ray."*

*June couldn't imagine going all in on the first boy she had a crush on. But she couldn't imagine Eleanor marrying Stan either.*

*"Ray's not here, is he?" Stan asked, his ears turning red as he glared at Harry. "And who knows if he'll ever come back? I might as well enjoy what he can't."*

*Stan started to approach Eleanor, but Harry moved into his way. Harry wasn't as tall or as old as Stan, but he stood his ground. "You stay away from her."*

*"Or what?" Stan said. "You going to stop me?"*

*"I will, if I have to." Harry breathed hard through his nose.*

*Eleanor's hands trembled as she set the New Year's sign down. "It's okay, Harry," she said as she walked up to him and touched his shoulder. "You don't need to do anything rash."*

*She took a deep breath and faced Stan. "I'm promised to Ray, and I'll wait for him forever, if I have to. Please stop asking me to marry you."*

*Stan's nostrils flared, and he threw the broom to the ground and left the depot, slamming the door shut behind him.*

*Harry's shoulders fell in apparent relief as he turned to Eleanor. "He's dangerous, Miss Eleanor. I'd stay away from him if I were you."*

*"I will, Harry, thank you."*

*With a nod, Harry left.*

*Eleanor picked up some more decorations, and June just stared at her.*

*"Are you okay?" June asked.*

*"No." Tears filled Eleanor's eyes. "If Ray were here, Stan wouldn't feel at liberty to talk to me the way he does."*

*"He doesn't mean anything by it." June tried to reassure Eleanor, but she didn't quite believe it herself. Stan meant every word he said to Eleanor. "That's why we should leave Dennison," she said, trying another tack. "Between Stan and Mabel treating you poorly and being reminded of Ray every time you turn around,*

you're miserable. Let's go to Washington. If you don't like it, we can always come back."

Eleanor's face calmed, and she slowly stopped trembling. "I suppose you're right."

"I know I'm right. I'll send a wire to the command center in Washington this afternoon and see if they have need of us. As soon as we know, we can leave Dennison and move in with Shannon."

A noise from outside the building made Eleanor jump, and she looked over her shoulder.

"Promise me you won't say anything to anyone," she said. "I don't want Stan to know where we're going."

"Are you afraid he'll come looking for you?"

Eleanor nodded. "He has nothing holding him here in Dennison either. The last thing I want is for him to follow us."

"I won't say anything," June promised. "No one needs to know where we're going."

"Okay," Eleanor agreed, "But I'm coming back if I don't like it."

"That's a deal." June couldn't hide her excitement. She'd agree to practically any stipulations Eleanor put on her if it meant she could get to Washington, DC.

January 6, 1944

June was sitting with Mrs. Snodgrass eating breakfast when she heard the mail drop through the slot in
the front door. She jumped up immediately, just as
she'd done all week, and ran for the hallway. She was
waiting for a reply from the Salvation Army, and if
she and Eleanor were going to keep their destination a
secret, she'd have to intercept any correspondence
from them before Mrs. Snodgrass saw it.

It had only been a week since she'd wired them,
but maybe they were desperate for help and would
answer soon.

"Mind your manners, Miss Manley," Mrs. Snodgrass
called behind her in her motherly voice. "No running in
the house."

June hardly paid attention to her kind landlady,
skidding to a halt on the freshly polished wood floors.
She picked up the scattered mail and thumbed through
it. Sure enough, there were two letters from the command center in Washington, DC. One was addressed
to her and one to Eleanor. She tore open her letter and
quickly scanned it, her heart pumping wildly.

They wanted her to come to Washington as soon as
possible to do clerical work.

"Anything important?" Mrs. Snodgrass called from the back of the house.

June wanted to shout for joy, but she remembered her promise to Eleanor that she wouldn't tell anyone where they were going. Eleanor had been a wreck this week, avoiding Stan at all costs. He'd asked her to marry him so many times, she'd lost count. Would he follow them to Washington if he knew where they were going? June didn't want to take that risk, so she couldn't even tell Mrs. Snodgrass her news. They'd have to find a way to sneak out of Dennison so no one would know where they'd gone. Stan would try to get it out of anyone who knew.

"Maybe," June said, trying to hide the joy in her voice. She wanted to run to the depot where Eleanor was already on duty and show her the letter, but she didn't want to make Mrs. Snodgrass suspicious. So she stuffed both letters into her handbag, put the rest of the mail on the hall table, and went back into the kitchen, where Mrs. Snodgrass dished up their plates. June and Eleanor were her only boarders at the moment, and Mr. Snodgrass had already left for work, so it was just the two of them.

The meal felt like it took hours but, in truth, only ten minutes passed before June gulped down her orange juice and told Mrs. Snodgrass she was heading to the depot.

"Your shift doesn't start for two more hours," Mrs. Snodgrass said.

"I thought I'd go early and see if they need extra help. The troop trains have been bigger than ever lately."

"Oh, how nice," Mrs. Snodgrass said.

June put on her hat, coat, mittens, and overshoes, grabbed her handbag, and headed toward the depot.

It was much colder today. A fresh blanket of snow made the roads slushy and difficult to navigate. It wasn't an ideal time to move to Washington, but it didn't matter to June. She had never been to a big city—not even Cleveland—and she was eager to get there. What would it be like? Reading the descriptions that Shannon had written had given her a good idea, but it was still so hard to imagine.

June had a feeling she would love the big city and never want to come back to Ohio.

Her excitement bubbled over by the time she reached the depot. She could hardly contain herself. How soon could she talk Eleanor into leaving? Would she be willing to go tonight? Or would that be too soon?

June pulled the letter out of her handbag, ready to give it to Eleanor the moment she found her.

"Have you seen Eleanor?" June asked Harry when she entered the depot.

Harry shook his head and glanced at the letter in June's hand. "Not for a while. Last I saw her, she was making sandwiches." He pointed to the letter. "Is that for Eleanor?"

June turned the front of the envelope to face her so Harry wouldn't see who it was from. She couldn't risk anyone knowing.

"Yes," she said.

He grinned, his brown eyes sparkling. "It looks official. Is it an important letter?"

June couldn't contain her excitement, and she nodded with a huge smile. "Very important."

Harry seemed just as pleased with the news as she was.

"I need to find Eleanor. I'll see you later, Harry."

"Okay." He started whistling a happy tune as she left him behind.

No one in the kitchen knew where Eleanor had gone, so she returned to the lobby. But there was no sign of her or Stan.

Concern tightened June's gut, and she walked quickly out to the platform. A biting wind hit her in the face, and she shivered. It was quiet out there, but when June looked to her right, she saw that Stan had Eleanor cornered. She was pressed against the wall, and he leaned up in front of her, keeping her pinned in place.

"Eleanor!" June called, running down the platform toward her friend.

Stan turned at the sound and scowled at June's arrival.

June scowled right back and glared at him until he walked away.

Eleanor crossed her arms over herself, tears in her eyes.

"What happened?" June asked her.

"I came out here to sweep, and he cornered me." She wiped her tears. "He wouldn't let me pass, even when I pushed against him." Eleanor wrapped her arms around June and hugged her tight. "I'm so happy you came when you did."

June hugged Eleanor back. "You need to tell someone that he's bullying you. Better yet"—she looked over her shoulder to make sure they were alone and handed Eleanor the unopened letter addressed to her—"we got accepted to work at the command center. They want us to come as soon as possible. Let's go tonight. We can take the midnight bus to Pittsburgh and bribe the ticket agent not to tell a soul. We'll catch a train heading to Washington from there. We don't need to tell anyone we're leaving, so Stan won't know where we've gone. We'll leave a note for Mrs. Snodgrass telling her that we're safe and we're together, and not to worry."

Eleanor bit her bottom lip, but June wouldn't let her have second thoughts.

"Don't even think about it," she said. "We need to get you away from Stan. Who knows what he would do if he cornered you, all alone, where no one could help you?"

Eleanor shivered. "Okay. Let's go tonight."

June grinned. "It's a plan."

"But, please," Eleanor said, "don't breathe a word about this to anyone. Stan scares me more than I let on. I don't want him to know anything."

"You have my word. I'll send a wire to my friend telling her we'll be in Washington by tomorrow afternoon. She'll be so excited."

"Are you sure she won't mind us staying with her?"

"It was her idea." June wanted to reassure Eleanor. "She'll be overjoyed. I promise."

Eleanor finally opened her letter and read it. "They want me to work in the office—and they're going to pay me."

June nodded. "Me too. We'll work together. And we'll make real money."

"We better, if we're going to take care of ourselves in Washington, DC." She shivered again. "It sounds like an awfully big place."

"Filled with countless servicemen," June added with a wiggle of her eyebrows.

"There's only one man for me," Eleanor reminded her.

June rolled her eyes playfully, but secretly, she hoped that a change of scenery would help Eleanor lighten up and put Ray in perspective. They'd been together only two weeks before he left six months ago. Surely, you couldn't fall in love in two weeks—could you? There had to be other men out there for Eleanor to focus her attention on, and June was going to help her find them.

# CHAPTER THIRTEEN

With only five days left before the grand opening, Debbie and Janet worked overtime to get the café ready. Thankfully, the space was air-conditioned, but Debbie still had to wipe the perspiration from her brow as she and Janet moved several boxes of supplies into the café from their cars.

Dale was hard at work in the restroom, and for the first time in two weeks, Debbie was hopeful that he could get it done in time.

"I just got a text," Janet said, her eyes lighting up as she set a box of napkins down. "Our display case is ready to be picked up."

Janet had found a curved glass display case from a bakery in New Philadelphia, and she'd had it refinished at a woodworking shop on the other side of town.

"How big is it?" Debbie asked.

"Too big to get into one of our cars." Janet bit her bottom lip. Today she wore a T-shirt that said I Sugarcoat Everything. "Do we know someone with a truck who can help us?"

The first person who came to mind was Greg, but Debbie didn't want to inconvenience him. "Greg has one—but he's probably busy."

"It would only take about thirty minutes to pick it up and drop it off. We could meet him there and help get it into his truck." She grinned. "I can bribe him with food."

"I don't know if we should bother him."

"It doesn't hurt to ask. Besides, I'd love to get it set up today. After work, Ian is going to bring our cash register too. All we'll need after that is our chairs."

Janet had found an antique cash register that had also needed a little refurbishment from an antique specialist in Uhrichsville. It would be ready after five, so Ian had agreed to pick it up for them.

"I guess it doesn't hurt to ask," Debbie conceded. "I'll text him and see if he has a little time."

Debbie pulled out her phone and sent Greg a quick text. As she was about to put her phone back in her pocket, it rang. And when she looked at the screen, Greg's name popped up.

"That was fast," Debbie said as she tapped the green icon. "Hi, Greg."

"Hey. I was sending another text when yours came in. I'd love to help you out. I actually have an hour for my lunch break, and I can leave right now. Are you ready?"

"We are. We can meet you there in about ten minutes—and then you'll have to let us treat you to lunch. Our fridge is stocked up, and I think we could whip together a sandwich or something simple."

"Sounds like a good trade. I'll see you soon."

As Janet drove them across town to meet Greg, Debbie remembered the letter they'd received from Susan the day before. It was still in her purse.

"In all the work today," she said to Janet, "I almost forgot about talking to Kim. I hope she can help us find information about Eleanor or June Manley at the Salvation Army Command Center in DC."

"Why don't you call her now?" Janet suggested. "While you're thinking about it."

"That's a good idea." Debbie found Kim's number on her cell phone and tapped the call icon then put it on speaker.

"Hey, Debbie," Kim said. "What can I do for you?"

Debbie quickly explained the letter from Eleanor to Mabel and that it had been written in March of 1944 on letterhead from the Salvation Army Command Center in Washington, DC. "I'm wondering if there's a way to get records from them or anything we can find about Eleanor O'Reilly and her friend, June Manley. I feel like we're getting closer to finding out what happened, but I still don't know why she didn't come back to Dennison after Ray returned."

"I'll contact the Salvation Army and see if they keep records like that," Kim promised. "And I'll do some more digging around here to see if I can find anything about a June Manley."

"Great. We really appreciate your help."

They said their goodbyes right as Janet pulled up outside the house where the display case waited for them. The man who had done the restoration operated out of his home. He had his garage door open, and there was the finished piece, looking brand-new.

Greg drove up in his truck seconds after they exited their car.

"Wow," Janet said to the man who had done the work. "This looks amazing, thank you."

"My pleasure."

As Janet wrote out a check, Debbie met up with Greg near his truck.

"Thank you for agreeing to help us, especially on such short notice," she said.

"Anytime." He smiled, revealing his dimples. "I'll help whenever I can. Don't be afraid to ask. Now that I'm done working on your house, I'll have to find other ways to see you."

The wind blew Debbie's hair, and she had to force it behind one ear as she returned his smile. He was flirting with her again—and, for a moment, she let herself revel in his teasing.

"How's the café coming along?" he asked, changing the subject quickly, for which she was grateful.

"Great. I think we're on track for the grand opening."

"Do you need any part-time servers?"

Debbie shrugged. "I'm not sure. It'll just be Janet and me at the beginning. She'll do all the baking and most of the cooking, and I'll serve and do the management end of things. We're only open for breakfast and lunch, so I think we can manage."

"If you're ever in need of part-time or temporary help, my mom, Paulette, would be a great person to ask. She was a waitress for most of her life and only recently retired—if you can call it that. She's probably busier than anyone else I know."

"Thank you. I'll keep that in mind." Debbie had wondered when, or if, they'd need to call in someone else to help. It was good to have a backup plan, in case she or Janet got sick or business was better than expected.

"We're ready to go," Janet said as she motioned for Greg and Debbie to come and help.

It wasn't easy, but with the four of them, and the use of a dolly that they borrowed, they were able to get the display case into Greg's truck. Hammer supervised every move from his perch in the cab.

Soon Janet and Debbie were back in Janet's car, heading toward the café.

"Greg made an offer," Debbie said. "His mom, Paulette, used to be a waitress, and he said we should call her if we need some extra help."

"I know Paulette," Janet said. "She has more energy than anyone else I know. She's helping Greg raise his boys, and she volunteers for many organizations in town. I think she knows everyone in Dennison."

"Would she be a good person to bring on, if we need the extra help?"

"She'd be a hoot to work with." Janet smiled. "I definitely think we should keep her in mind. It might be nice to have someone on call."

"That's what I was thinking." It was one less thing to worry about, and for that Debbie was grateful.

When they returned to the depot, Jaxon and Julian were there waiting with their bikes.

"I called in reinforcements," Greg said as he jumped out of his truck. "I would hate to see this case get damaged, so I thought the boys could help us take it into the café. I hope you don't mind feeding a couple extra mouths."

"Not at all. We're happy for the help," Janet said with a grin.

It didn't take long for the five of them to get the case off the truck and into the café. Janet showed them where she wanted it, and Greg helped them to level it and plug it into the outlet on the floor underneath. Soon the light in the case turned on, and the five of them stood back to admire it.

"I really like what you've done in here," Greg said as he looked around. "It has a homey atmosphere. I can see this becoming a favorite spot for locals."

Debbie surveyed the room, looking at it through Greg's eyes, and she liked what she saw.

"How would you like some grilled cheese sandwiches?" Janet asked the boys. "I also have some tomato bisque soup I can heat up for you."

"That sounds perfect," Greg answered for him and his sons. "We'll take whatever you've got."

"Coming right up." Janet disappeared into the kitchen while the boys took seats at the counter. Hammer dropped to the floor under their stools with a big doggie groan.

"You guys are our first customers," Debbie said.

"That's quite an honor." Greg took a seat next to his boys. "I'm sure we won't be your last."

"Let's hope not." Debbie smiled. "What would you like to drink?"

"I'll take a Coke," Greg said.

The boys told Debbie what they wanted, and she went into the kitchen to get it for them.

Janet was in there, an apron tied around her waist and a smile on her face. She had a skillet warming up on the stove, and most of her ingredients on the stainless-steel counter. "I can't wait to start doing this for real."

"Next week at this time, it will be real." Debbie was excited too. The fulfillment of her dream to come home to Dennison and open up a café was just five days away.

Later that day, after Debbie had left the café, she decided to stop by the Good Shepherd Retirement Center to see Ray and take a few more items she'd found in the house to him. It was getting close to suppertime, so she hoped he wouldn't be eating yet, because she also wanted to ask him a few more questions. The letter from Eleanor was in her purse, and she hoped to find out whether he knew she went to Washington, DC.

The smell of tacos was in the air as Debbie walked down the hall to Ray's room, holding the cardboard box she'd found tucked back in one of the closets. It was full of black-and-white pictures, and she thought Ray might want them.

She was still full from the delicious grilled cheese sandwich Janet had made for lunch, but she was already thinking about her own supper later that evening. She planned to finish unpacking boxes and start getting her house ready for her guests, who were coming Friday evening.

Ray's bedroom door was open, and he had a guest. Eileen Palmer sat across from him at a small table, and they were playing a game of chess.

"Hello," Debbie said as she stood at the open door. "Mind if I come in?"

"Debbie!" Ray's face lit up as if she were his long-lost grand-daughter. "Come on in."

"You're just in time to see me beat Ray—again," Eileen said. She moved her queen and said, "Checkmate!"

Ray frowned as he studied the board. Finally, he leaned back and crossed his arms. "I don't know why I keep playing with you. Remind me to say no next time you ask."

There was a sparkle in Eileen's eyes as she looked at her opponent. "You've been threatening to quit playing with me since we were children, and you haven't yet."

Ray's frown turned into a grin, and he looked decades younger. "That's because I'll beat you one of these days. That's why I've lived this long, you know, just so I can beat you at least once."

A sweet moment passed between the pair, and Debbie imagined that these two friends had seen a lot together over the years. Or were they more than friends?

"What brings you all the way out here?" Ray asked as he turned to look at Debbie. "I hope good news."

"I have some news—though I don't know if it's good." Debbie handed him the box. "I found this tucked into the back of a closet upstairs under the eaves. I thought you might like it."

Ray's eyes lit up. "I should have moved years ago. I would have found all these things a lot earlier." He removed the box lid and shook his head in wonder. "I bought a Kodak camera a few months before I joined the army, and I took it along with me to Europe."

Debbie took a seat and watched as he sifted through the images, commenting here or there as he showed them to her and Eileen.

His hand paused over the box, and Debbie glanced up to see a look on his face. Wonder, amazement, and grief all seemed to mingle in his gaze.

Eileen studied Ray's face as well. "Eleanor?" she asked.

Ray nodded as he lifted a picture out of the box and stared at it for a long time.

Neither Debbie nor Eileen spoke.

Finally, Ray offered the picture to Debbie.

It was a photo of a young man and woman, their arms around each other, smiling at the camera. The man wore a pair of jeans, rolled at the ankles, with a button-down shirt. The woman was in a dress with heels. She had a ribbon tied around her head.

"That's Eleanor and me," Ray said, his voice breaking. "A week before I left Dennison."

Eleanor was very beautiful, and though it was a black-and-white picture, it was clear to see that she had blond hair and very light eyes. "She's stunning," Debbie said.

"That's what I always thought," Ray said. "I couldn't understand why she liked me."

"You look like a young Gregory Peck," Debbie said. She loved watching old movies, and the ones from the 1940s were some of her favorites.

Eileen smiled and nodded. "Ray was the cutest boy in town, but he was three years younger than me, so he was just a kid in my eyes." Her smile turned a bit wistful. "Eventually age doesn't matter though."

Ray was still looking at the picture and didn't seem to hear what Eileen had said. "We were very much in love," he said. "All these years later, it still hurts like it did in 1944 when she stopped writing to me, and then when I came home and she was gone…"

"I have something for you." Debbie reached into her purse. "Eleanor wrote a letter to Mabel Thomas in March 1944. There might be a helpful clue in here."

Ray looked up quickly and took the letter from Debbie. He scanned it, frowning.

"What is she talking about?" he asked. "Why would Eleanor believe that she wasn't good enough for me? It was the other way around." He looked to Eileen to confirm his comment, but she was gazing down at her hands.

"And who is June?" he asked. "I don't know anyone named June."

"Don't you remember?" Eileen asked. "I told you that June Manley disappeared with Eleanor on the same day."

"I don't remember you telling me about a woman named June," Ray said to her. He looked at the letter again. "And they went to the Salvation Army Command Center in Washington, DC? I didn't know that either. Why didn't Eleanor tell me?"

"This is the first I've heard it too," Eileen said.

"And what about this?" Ray continued. "She says she agrees with June that she can't be the wife I need now? Why was it impossible? And why didn't she want me to come for her?" He looked like he was about to dash off to Washington to search for her now.

"I don't know," Debbie said. "We're trying to find records about Eleanor and June from the Salvation Army. If I learn anything else, I'll let you know immediately."

"And this," Ray said, pointing to the paper. "What events were out of her control and preventing her from fulfilling her promise to me? She says she loves me, so why couldn't she have told me what happened? I would have married her, no matter what the circumstances. If she'd only known that I would wait eighty years for her, never loving another woman—would that have changed her mind?"

His words seemed to trouble Eileen, who continued to stare at her hands, sadness weighing down her features.

Ray's voice was desperate and weak as he spoke, though neither Debbie nor Eileen could answer his questions.

"When was the last time Eleanor wrote to you?" Debbie asked. "Did she write after she left Dennison?"

"The last letter she sent me was dated January 5, 1944, from here in Dennison. I have all of her letters. Would you like to see them?" He set the letter and cardboard box of photos on the chessboard and wheeled himself over to a dresser. He opened the bottom drawer, tugged out a shoebox, and set it on his lap. When he returned to Debbie, he opened the box and took out a handful of letters, all tied together with frayed twine.

"This is the last letter she wrote to me," Ray said as he handed over the yellow envelope. It looked like it had been handled a thousand times. The writing was faded, and the seams of the envelope were falling apart.

"You don't mind if I read it?" Debbie asked.

"Please. If it helps us find Eleanor, I don't care if you read all of them."

Debbie slowly opened the envelope and pulled out the letter. By now, she was familiar with the handwriting, but this letter was far different than the one Eleanor had written to Mabel just two and a half months later.

# CHAPTER FOURTEEN

*January 5, 1944*

*Dear Ray,*

*I can hardly believe you've been gone over six months. It feels like so much longer. Life in Dennison hasn't changed any since you went away. Each day feels longer than the next, and I wonder how I'll survive until you return. Will I be an old woman? Will you still love me? I know I'll love you. Nothing could change that.*

*The troop trains are still coming through, and sometimes I wonder where all those men are coming from. Thousands go by each week, and they all make me think of you. I know it's silly, but I look for you in each of their faces. I long to see you again, even if only for a moment. I look at your picture dozens of times a day, and though I have it memorized, I'm so afraid I'll* forget what you look like or what your voice sounds like, or how my hand fit so perfectly in yours.

I wish I knew where you were stationed. I try to read all the newspapers, hoping and praying you aren't staying where the fighting is the worst, but it just makes me sad. When I start feeling like that, I pull out one of your letters and read that instead. You always make me laugh, even when you're working so hard. You find a way to be joyful, and that makes me want to be joyful too. I love that about you. I only wish we could have known each other longer, so I had more memories to recall.

As for news at the depot, Eileen hired someone to take over your job. He hates the work, and I'm afraid everyone compares him to you constantly. He could never live up to you, though, and we all know it. I do not like him and wish he would leave, but Harry is still working at the depot, and so are Eileen and many of the others you know. There is also another girl boarding with the Snodgrasses. She's funny and adventurous, but she doesn't like hearing me talk about you so much. What she doesn't know is that even when I'm not talking about you, I'm thinking about you.

But I don't want to talk about anyone else. Not now. I am about to go to sleep, and I want to think of you and you alone. I want to dream about the home we'll share together, the children we'll have, the happy memories we'll make. Can you see the future, Ray? I can, and it's lovely. But I don't always think of the life we'll have. Sometimes I think about a single day. If I had you back for just one day, I'd pack a picnic basket and take you down to the Tuscarawas River and revel in the beauty of your company. I'd sing to you, and you could read to me. It would be marvelous.

Sometimes I do dream of you, Ray, and I'm so happy. My arms long to hold you again, and my eyes ache to see you. I hope and pray it will be soon, my love. And, until that day, I pray you are safe.

Don't forget me, Ray. Someday soon, we will be together again, and we will have a beautiful life.

I love you.

Eleanor

*January 7, 1944*

Union Station was crowded as Eleanor descended from the train. The trip from Dennison to Washington had been longer than she expected, and she hadn't been able to sleep well. They'd left Dennison by bus at midnight and transferred to a train in Pittsburgh, *arriving in DC at noon. Her eyelids felt like gravel, her head pounded, and her throat burned with the need to drink something cool.*

*"We should go to the Salvation Army Command Center first," June said as she came off the train behind Eleanor. June looked refreshed and ready to tackle the day. Her hair was perfectly coiffed, her lipstick was pristine, and her eyes were clear. "After we check in with them, we can find my friend Shannon's house. It's not too far away—I don't think."*

*The noise in the depot was overwhelming, and the press of people was mind-boggling to Eleanor. She'd never seen anything like it in her life. Not even when the troop trains unloaded in Dennison.*

*This was another level of crowded. Both men and women jostled each other to get out of the way. People pushed and prodded Eleanor from every side, and no matter which way she turned, she was in someone's path. As they climbed the stairs into the central room, her mouth fell open at the immense dome over her head. She hadn't known such places existed. She was eager to get out of the station, but she wasn't looking forward to the frigid air outside.*

*"This way, I think," June said as she took Eleanor's hand and pulled her toward the steps leading out of the*

station. "Hold tight to your bag. You don't want anyone to steal it."

Eleanor clutched her suitcase in her sweating
hand. All of her worldly possessions were in her bag,
including her letters and pictures of Ray.

They pushed and clawed to get out of the station and
made their way to the bright street. The sun hurt Eleanor's
eyes, and she squinted to see, putting her free hand up to
shade her view. Her breath froze as it left her mouth.

For a moment, they just stopped and stared at the
city around them. Eleanor had never known there were
so many people in the world. Where were they all going?
Back home, she rarely passed a person without acknowl-
edging them—but here? Everyone moved so quickly,
hardly looking up. No one acknowledged anyone else.

And the cars! They moved in a steady stream every
which way. Horns honked, people shouted, and the
smell of exhaust filled the air around her, making her
headache even worse.

There was so much to distract her, the cold didn't
bother her as much as she thought it would.

"Look there," June said with excitement. "I think
that's the US Capitol building."

Eleanor looked, and she couldn't believe her eyes.
But it seemed so far away. Everything felt so far.

"Excuse me," June said to a stranger as he passed by. "Which way to the Salvation Army Command Center?"

The man seemed surprised that she would stop him, but when he got his bearings, he shrugged. "I don't know where that is."

"It's on Pennsylvania Avenue." She told him the address.

"That's a good five miles from here."

"F-five miles?" Eleanor stammered, wondering if she'd have the energy to walk that far.

After the man told them the best route, June stared in the direction he had pointed, appearing to calculate what it would take. She finally said, "Should we start?"

There was no other choice. They'd used almost all their money to purchase their bus and train tickets to the city, and Eleanor only had about a dollar left of the inheritance she'd received from her parents. She would need it to buy food until she could get paid for her new job.

They walked for several minutes, not saying a word to each other. Eleanor didn't think she could form a sentence, even if she wanted to. She was too over-whelmed, and not in a good way. With each step she took, this decision felt more and more foolish. She could have stayed in Dennison and had a nice place to live until Ray came home. The Snodgrasses didn't charge her anything to board with them, because she volunteered at the canteen. But here, she was all on her own. No one cared if she was fed or housed. It was her—and June—against the world.

At least she had June.

Eleanor's feet began to ache with the cold, and her head pounded more and more, but there was no way to stop now. They needed to get the meeting with the Salvation Army people over with so they could find Shannon's house and get a good night's rest. That was all she needed. Some sleep. Things would look better in the morning.

It took almost two hours, but they finally arrived at the large brick building with the familiar Salvation Army sign out front. Eleanor was shivering and irritable, while June grinned from ear to ear.

"Isn't this exciting?" she asked, taking in their surroundings with a big, contented sigh. "I know I'm going to love it here."

Eleanor wished she could say the same, but she already knew how she felt about the big city. It wasn't for her. She felt small, insignificant, and lonely. She'd spent years alone, without family or friends, and now she realized that the people in Dennison had become the only family and friends she knew. Why had she agreed to let June take her away from there?

Immediately thoughts of Stan came to mind, and a shiver went up Eleanor's spine. Stan had told her that he would stop at nothing to get her to marry him. No matter how much she protested, he wouldn't leave her alone. She was afraid people would start to think she enjoyed his attention. She'd considered telling Eileen, but she didn't want to cause trouble. Stan was getting paid to be at the depot, but Eleanor was not. Better to just leave, for now, and wait for Ray here in the city. Maybe she'd grow to like it here, and it wouldn't last forever. One day soon, Ray would come back, and they would start their life together.

Until then, she needed to stay as far away from Stan as she could, and Washington, DC was as good a place as any.

Besides, if she wanted to try and make it in New York City someday, she'd have to get used to all the people and the noise.

They eventually found their supervisor and filled out the paperwork necessary to begin work the next day. Eleanor's hands shook as she filled out the forms, and her headache would not ease up.

When they were finally done, Eleanor breathed a sigh of relief and left the building with June.

"It might take us a little longer to get to Shannon's house," June said. "I'm not quite sure where it is, but I know it's on the river and somewhere in Alexandria."

Eleanor wanted to groan.

After June made some inquiries, they realized Shannon lived almost nine miles away.

"I know we don't have much money," Eleanor said, never feeling so tired in her life, "but maybe we could take a streetcar." She didn't want to complain or whine, but she was exhausted. "Do you mind?"

June looked at Eleanor for the first time since arriving in the city—really looked at her—and frowned. "Your face is all red, Eleanor." She put her hand to Eleanor's forehead. "And you're burning up. How long have you felt like this?"

"Just before we pulled into Union Station." She pushed June's hand away. "I'll be fine once I can get some sleep and something to drink. I'd like to write to Ray tonight and tell him where I've gone."

Concern tightened June's face, and she looked left and right. "We'll find a streetcar and get you to Shannon's as soon as we can. I want you in bed and resting."

June took control again, and soon they were on a streetcar, heading toward South Union Street where Shannon lived.

The moment Shannon's mother saw Eleanor, she took her under her wing like her own child. She was kind and thoughtful and tucked Eleanor into the guest room bed with warm chicken soup and tea with lemon and honey.

Eleanor missed having a mother, and for a few glorious moments, she reveled in the attention from this woman she'd just met. But despite her deep thirst and hunger, the raging headache and exhaustion were too much for her. She didn't even finish her soup or tea before she started to doze off.

The kind woman who had taken her in chuckled as she tucked the blankets closer around Eleanor.

It was the last moment of laughter Eleanor heard for a long, long time.

# CHAPTER FIFTEEN

It was hard for Debbie to sleep after visiting with Ray and Eileen. She kept thinking that the whole situation with Eleanor's disappearance could have been avoided if Eleanor had simply written to Ray. Told him where she went and what happened. No matter what it was, surely true love would have conquered all.

At least, that was what the fairy tales told her.

But true love hadn't conquered all for Debbie, a thought that kept her up most of the night. She still mourned for Reed, though it felt like that part of her life had happened to someone else. Once in a while the memories hit her with a strength she didn't see coming, and she would be overcome with the event that had robbed her of so much happiness.

It was a new day, and since she hadn't been able to sleep much, Debbie decided to leave her house early and walk to the café. The day was fresh and vibrant, with a brilliant blue sky, birds singing from the trees, and sunshine sparkling on everything it touched. Once the café opened to the public, Janet would plan to get there around four to start baking for the day. Debbie would arrive at six to open the restaurant at seven and start waiting tables. But, for today, they had decided to start at nine. Their cups, dinnerware, and cutlery were supposed to arrive today and would need to be cleaned and sorted. The commercial coffee maker was also coming, as was a shipment of vintage candy Debbie had ordered. Everything would need to be stocked and organized.

She could hardly believe they were so close to the grand opening. Just four more days.

Debbie's phone began to vibrate in her back pocket. She pulled it out and frowned when she saw the number. It wasn't one she recognized, but she'd been getting a lot of phone calls from vendors and service technicians lately, so she decided to answer it.

"Hello?"

"Hi. Is this Debbie Albright?"

"Yes."

"This is Eleanor Pantzke, responding to your message."

Debbie stopped walking, excited and a little nervous to hear from her. "Thank you for calling me, Eleanor. I know I must have taken you by surprise."

"A little, but I often thought my father's past would catch up with me." She chuckled. "And please, call me Ellie. Everyone does."

"Was he a troublemaker, Ellie?" Debbie laughed, trying to keep the conversation light, though Harry hadn't held back about the kind of man Stan Schroeder had been.

"Let's just say that he lived a wild life before he met my mother, but she seemed to straighten him out."

Her mother? Was her mother Eleanor O'Reilly? "What was your mother's name?"

Debbie held her breath as she waited for Ellie's reply.

"Her name was Pamela Stone. He met her about a year after he came to Columbus—at least, that's what he told me. My mother died when I was very young, and it was just my father who raised me."

"I'm so sorry to hear that. As I said in my message, I'm looking for information about a woman named Eleanor O'Reilly. She worked with your father in Dennison. Do you know anything about her?"

"I do, actually." Ellie's voice was clear, though touched with age. "I was named after her, as you probably guessed. Dad didn't tell me that until after my mom died, because he didn't want to hurt her feelings. He used to talk about Eleanor O'Reilly all the time, although he never told me where he knew her from. Said she could sing like an angel and that if she hadn't been engaged to another man, he would have convinced her to marry him."

"Did he ever tell you what happened to her?"

"He didn't know, but I did a little research a few years ago, and I learned more."

Again, Debbie paused. "What did you learn?"

"That she became a flight nurse and served for just six months before her plane went down in April, 1945, near Eschwege, Germany."

Debbie's mouth slipped open as she listened to the story. "Are you sure?"

"Yes, I'm afraid so. I did some extensive research back in the 1970s. It wasn't easy to find her. I've kept all my notes and documents. I have them, if you'd like to see them sometime." She paused for a moment. "My daughter comes every weekend to see me, and she could make copies or whatever they do these days to send documents to people. Would that work?"

"That would be wonderful," Debbie said. A heaviness settled on her chest as she thought about how sad Ray would be to learn that Eleanor had died in an airplane accident. It surprised her that Eleanor had gone on to become a nurse—a flight nurse at that—but it might explain why he couldn't find her. Maybe he hadn't been looking for her in the army.

"Thank you so much for all your help," she said, gathering her roaming thoughts.

"You're welcome. I'm happy to be able to help."

Debbie ended the call and continued walking toward the café. It didn't make any sense to her that Eleanor would become a flight nurse and not tell Ray. What had happened between January 1944, when Eleanor had gone to Washington, and March 1944, when she had sent Mabel a letter telling her that she couldn't return to Ray—and then April 1945, when she died as a flight nurse in Germany?

Something wasn't adding up, and Debbie was determined to get to the bottom of it.

She was still mulling over the information she'd just been given as she entered the café a few minutes later. The smell of coffee immediately filled her nose as she inhaled a big whiff. Janet was there, sitting at the counter with a steaming mug and several invoices in front of her.

"Good morning," Janet said. "Coffee is hot, if you'd like some."

Debbie walked up to the coffee maker and poured herself a cup. "I need a little pick-me-up after last night."

"What happened?" Janet looked up as she took a sip from her mug.

"I didn't sleep well." Debbie joined Janet at the counter. "And you'll never believe it, but I just got a call from Stan Schroeder's daughter, Eleanor—Ellie."

"Oh?" Janet sat up a little straighter. "What did she have to say?"

"She told me that she did her own research and discovered that Eleanor O'Reilly became a flight nurse and served for six months before dying in an airplane crash in Germany in 1945."

"What?" Janet set her coffee down and gave Debbie an incredulous look. "Are you serious?"

"That's what she told me. But it doesn't make any sense. Why would Eleanor not tell Ray where she was before she died?" She shook her head. "I think something huge happened right when she got to DC, and because of it she was either too embarrassed or ashamed to tell Ray, and then her life took a complete shift and she decided to become a nurse."

"Nothing we've learned about her so far would indicate that she had dreams of becoming a nurse—right?"

"Right. All I know is that she wanted to be a singer, wanted to marry Ray, and ended up leaving Dennison with June Manley to work in Washington, DC as a secretary. None of that would indicate she wanted to be a nurse. But who knows what the war could have done to her? Maybe she felt a calling to do something to help."

The bell over the door rang, and both Debbie and Janet looked up to find Harry poking his head into the café with Crosby at his side.

"Good morning, ladies," Harry said with a big grin. "I know you're not open until next week, but I couldn't help but smell that delicious coffee aroma wafting out of here. I was wondering if you might have an extra cup I could buy."

"Come on in, Harry," Debbie said as she motioned him and Crosby into the café. "Do you know Janet?"

"Sure I do," Harry said with a grin. "Janet and I have known each other for years."

"It's nice to see you again, Harry," Janet said. "And you too, Crosby." She patted the dog on the head. "Crosby looks like he could use some breakfast. I was about to make some eggs and toast. Would you two like some?"

"Well now," Harry said as he took a seat on a stool at the head of the counter. "If you're going to make some, I won't say no."

"I'll be just a minute," Janet said.

"And I'll get you some coffee," Debbie added. She took a mug off the shelf and poured a cup for Harry.

He took it and inhaled deeply before taking his first sip. "Mmm. That sure hits the spot. This is the best coffee I've had all day."

Debbie laughed and took a sip of her own.

"I hope I wasn't interrupting an important conversation," Harry said. "You and Janet looked like you were in a serious discussion when I walked in."

"We were talking about Eleanor O'Reilly," Debbie said. "I just learned today that she became a flight nurse and died in Germany in 1945."

"Eleanor O'Reilly? A flight nurse?" Harry frowned. "That doesn't sound right."

"That's what I thought too."

"Did you find this out on the internet?" Harry asked.

Debbie shook her head. "No, this was information that someone found in the 1970s."

"Maybe the internet has updated information," he said.

"You know, you might be right. I haven't even looked Eleanor up online. That should have been the first thing I did."

"Do you have your phone?" Harry smiled. "I sure do like those inventions. Can't think what my daddy would say if he saw what we carried around in our back pockets. He couldn't even imagine something like that."

"It is pretty amazing." Debbie pulled out her phone and typed *Eleanor O'Reilly Eschwege Germany 1945.*

The first link that appeared said, *Together We Served—First Lieutenant Eleanor O'Reilly.*

"There *is* something about her," Debbie said, excitement in her voice. She tapped on the link and came around the counter to show Harry the article.

A picture of First Lieutenant Eleanor O'Reilly appeared, and both Debbie and Harry sat up straighter.

"That's not our Eleanor," Harry said. "I don't know who that woman is."

Debbie read the rest of the article. "This Eleanor O'Reilly was thirty years old, and she was from Texas, not Ohio."

"Our Eleanor would have only been twenty in 1945," Harry said. "You got the wrong information, Debbie. Where did you hear about this Eleanor?"

"From Stan Schroeder's daughter. Her name is Eleanor as well." Debbie shook her head. "I'll need to call her and tell her she found the wrong woman. She wasn't named after the woman who died in Germany."

"Is there anything else on the internet about our Eleanor?" Harry asked, his face hopeful.

Debbie scrolled through all the links, but she couldn't find anything about Eleanor O'Reilly from New Philadelphia, Ohio.

"I'm afraid our Eleanor didn't leave much of a trail. I'm still waiting to hear from Kim to see if the Salvation Army has any information about her or June Manley."

"I hope they do. They might be our last chance."

Debbie couldn't agree more.

A few minutes later, Janet came out of the kitchen with her hands full. She had a plate of eggs and toast for Debbie, one for Harry, and one for Crosby.

"You're going to spoil him," Harry warned Janet as she set Crosby's eggs and toast in front of him.

"I don't mind," Janet said. "Everyone deserves a good breakfast."

"We might just be here every morning," Harry said with a laugh. "Service like this isn't found every day."

"We'll love to have you," Debbie assured him as she dug into her eggs.

"Our first regular customer," Janet added. "Or should I say, customers?" She looked down at Crosby, but he was so busy eating, he didn't seem to notice.

Debbie quickly filled Janet in on the information they found about the flight nurse, and Janet nodded.

"At least we know we were on the wrong trail," she said. "We won't waste our time waiting for misinformation."

"I suppose you're right," Debbie said. Though she was happy that it wasn't the Eleanor O'Reilly they were looking for, she still didn't know what happened to the right one.

# CHAPTER SIXTEEN

It wasn't until Wednesday that Debbie started to get really nervous about the grand opening. As she stood in the café, looking at all the tables without chairs and listening to Dale work in the restroom, she shook her head in exasperation. Would they be ready on time?

Janet was in the kitchen baking cookies, which they would offer with lemonade as free refreshments for anyone who came to the grand opening to check them out and say hello. The smell filled the café and made Debbie's stomach growl, but she didn't have time to stop and savor the goodies.

"Dale?" Debbie called as she approached the restroom.

The older man was in the one-stall bathroom painting the walls a soft creamy yellow. Trim still needed to be hung, and the tile still needed to be laid. And the drain had not yet been delivered, so the sink wasn't working.

"What can I do for you?" Dale asked as he set the roller on the tray.

"The grand opening is on Saturday," Debbie said, trying to keep her voice pleasant. "That gives us just two more workdays after today. Do you think the restroom will be ready?"

"Two days is plenty of time," he said. "I'll finish up the painting today, lay the tile tomorrow, and get the trim work done on Friday."

"And what about the drain?"

Dale scratched his whiskered chin and shrugged. "I can't do anything about the mail. Hopefully it comes in time and I'll have it installed."

It wasn't a big restroom, but Debbie knew that tiling a floor and hanging trim could be time-consuming.

"Do you need any extra help? My dad said he could stop by—"

"I got it under control." Dale surveyed the room, speaking slow and easy. "I've got a few men I could pull off another crew if I need to, but I know I can get this done on my own."

Dale's workers had helped get the other projects done in the café, but for whatever reason, when it came to the restroom, he worked alone.

"Okay," Debbie said, slowly, trying hard to trust him. "Let me know if you run into a snag and need more help."

"Will do." Dale was good-natured, and nothing seemed to fluster him.

Debbie wished she could say the same about herself.

She left the restroom and returned to the main part of the café, scanning the room to see if anything needed to be done. The vintage candy she had ordered was now organized on a shelf near the antique cash register. There was Black Jack and Teaberry chewing gum, Atomic Fireballs, Banana Split taffy, Cherry Mash, Boston Baked Beans, Necco wafers, and more. The bakery display case was set up and ready for the first batch of goodies Janet would bake on Saturday morning before the grand opening. The counter shone, the stools anchored to the floor.

Harry had seemed to favor the first stool, and they affectionately told him it was his for the taking. He'd been back that morning for coffee, eggs, and toast, Crosby alongside him. The last Debbie saw, he had returned to his favorite seat on the platform to watch the trains. It was nice to have their first regular customer.

The doorbell jingled, and Debbie smiled when she saw Kim enter the café holding a folder.

"Good morning," Debbie said. "Care for a cup of coffee?"

"I'd love one." Kim held up the folder. "I brought some great news for you."

Debbie's pulse picked up speed, and she motioned for Kim to have a seat at the counter. "I'll get Janet. I'm sure she'll want to hear this."

After Debbie told Janet that Kim was there, she grabbed a mug and poured Kim a cup of coffee.

"You have good news?" Janet asked as she came out of the kitchen with a smile, wiping flour off her hands with a dish towel.

"I was able to speak to the archivist at the Salvation Army headquarters in Washington, DC," Kim explained as she opened her file. "I gave her the names Eleanor O'Reilly and June Manley, with a start date of 1943. I received this yesterday." Kim handed them a couple of sheets of paper.

"What is it?" Debbie asked.

"It's June Manley's journal—or, at least, a few pages of one journal she kept. It turns out that it was much easier to find information on June, because she worked for the Salvation Army her entire life, eventually becoming a major and serving all over the world. Upon her death, her family donated her journals to the Salvation Army archives, because much of what she wrote about centered around her work."

"And what is this?" Janet asked, indicating the paper she held.

"This is a portion of June's journal from 1950. It mentions Eleanor O'Reilly, so the archivist sent me photocopies. She thought they'd be helpful in our search, and they are. Take a look."

Debbie found the beginning of the entry, dated July 17, 1950, and began to read.

> *Today took me by surprise. I ran into an old friend and roommate I had not seen in over five years. Eleanor O'Reilly was a dear woman I met in Dennison, Ohio, at the Salvation Army canteen. We came to Washington, DC together and worked in the same office for over a year. When I was transferred to the office in San Francisco in 1945 at the end of the war, I lost touch with her. We wrote back and forth for a couple of years, but our correspondence slowly faded. I didn't realize she was still working in Washington! Imagine my surprise to find her there when I came into town on business.*
>
> *When we were in Dennison, Eleanor was engaged to be married to a serviceman that she was crazy about. I was jealous of her happiness, I suppose, and encouraged her to come with me to expand her horizons and forget about him. In a way, I suppose that's exactly what happened.*
>
> *When I bumped into her today, I was so happy to see that she has made a good life for herself. I do believe it has a lot to do with the man she is planning to marry in two weeks. His name is Harrison Jones. He's a veteran and came to work for*

*the Salvation Army after being medically discharged. Eleanor said it took her a long time to let herself fall in love again. She said that she finally accepted the reality that her fiancé, Ray, had probably married his childhood sweetheart, Mabel, years before, and it was time for her to move on.*

*This evening, I met Eleanor and Harrison for supper, and I was so happy to see that they are truly in love. Harrison is so handsome, and Eleanor is such a beauty. Harrison said the war will always be a part of their story and that the physical reminders of their limitations keeps them humble. He said we must never forget the great sacrifices of an entire nation to preserve our freedom.*

*They are planning to return to his hometown of Cameron, West Virginia, to open a little gas station and hopefully start a family. I have to admit, I was jealous of Eleanor's happiness, but again, if anyone deserves it, it's her, after all she's been through. I wished them well and told them how happy I was to have bumped into Eleanor again. I hope and pray they have a truly joyful life together.*

The journal entry ended, and Debbie sat there for a few seconds to let it all sink in.

"She thought Ray married Mabel." Janet shook her head.

"But at least we know that she was happy, in the end," said Kim. "That's not nothing."

"We can look to see if she lived in Cameron, West Virginia," Janet said. "Maybe she has family members who are still there and can tell us more about her life."

"You're right." Debbie's excitement mounted again. "We finally have a real lead and know where she ended up."

Her cell phone was sitting on the counter, so she grabbed it and opened an internet browser. She typed in *Eleanor O'Reilly Jones Cameron West Virginia.*

A Whitepages link immediately appeared, and Debbie's eyes opened wide. "According to this, it says that Eleanor Jones is still living in Cameron, West Virginia!"

"What?" Janet stepped closer to Debbie to look at the phone. "Where does it say that?"

"Right here." Debbie pointed to it. "There's a phone number too."

"Do you seriously think she's still alive?" Janet looked up at Debbie, her eyes wide with curiosity and surprise.

"There's only one way to find out." Debbie tapped the phone number, and it immediately began to ring. She put the phone on speaker so her friends could hear the conversation.

"Hello?" answered a young woman.

"Hello," Debbie said, her nerves jumbled together. "May I speak to Eleanor?"

"Granny's sleeping right now," the woman said. "Can I take a message?"

Did that mean Eleanor was, in fact, alive? Elation washed over Debbie. Cameron, West Virginia, was less than two hours away. It was easily within driving distance. If Eleanor was alive, they could go see her.

"My name is Debbie Albright. I live in Dennison, Ohio, where your grandmother lived and worked for a short time. I've been trying to locate her for a friend who has been looking for her for almost eighty years."

"My goodness," the woman said. "That's a long time to look for someone."

"I agree, and now that I've found her, you can imagine how happy that will make him."

"My name is Connie," the woman said. "Eleanor is actually my great-grandmother. I live with her and am her full-time caregiver."

"I'm very glad to talk to you, Connie," Debbie said. "I'm wondering, is Eleanor able to travel? I know my friend would love to see her again."

"Can I ask who your friend is?"

"His name is Raymond Zink, and I believe he and your grandmother were sweethearts during World War II. I think they might have even been engaged to be married at one point. What I've heard is that Eleanor promised Ray she'd be waiting for him to return, but when he got back from the war, he was never able to locate her."

"Ray?" Connie asked, her voice lilting with familiarity.

"Yes. I bought his house and found an old record that Eleanor had recorded for him. When I took it to him at his retirement home, he asked me to help him find her."

"I've heard all about Raymond Zink," Connie said. "Granny never forgot him. And it doesn't surprise me that she made him a record. She's sung to me all my life."

"He never forgot about her either." Debbie looked up at Janet and Kim and smiled. There were tears in Janet's eyes, which she wiped away with her apron.

"Do you think she would be willing to see him?" Debbie asked Connie. "I know he would love to see her again."

There was a pause, and then Connie said, "My granny is very weak, and she's been declining fast. We've begun hospice care for her, and though her mind is still sharp at ninety-eight, her body is not cooperating. Each day is a miracle that she's still alive. I can't promise that she'll make it till you can get here."

Debbie looked up and saw her concern mirrored in Kim's and Janet's faces.

"Do you think she'd be up for a visit from Ray?" Debbie asked. "If we could get him to her in time?"

"She's been seeing family and close friends, when she's able," Connie said. "I think she would love to see Ray one last time. But you'll need to get him here as soon as possible."

When Debbie looked at Janet, Janet nodded.

"Would tomorrow be soon enough?" It was already later in the day, and they were two hours away.

"I'm not sure—I hope so."

"We will try our very hardest to get him there," Debbie promised. "We'll get there around ten, if he's available."

"That should work for us," Connie agreed. "I don't think I'll tell Granny that Ray is coming. She likes surprises, and I'd love to help give her this one. Perhaps the best one of her life."

After Connie gave her their address, Debbie said, "I look forward to meeting you tomorrow, Connie."

"I look forward to meeting you too, Debbie." She paused again. "I can't wait to meet Ray. I've always wondered about him. Granddaddy used to tease Granny about Raymond Zink. Granddaddy knew that

Granny loved him and had devoted her life to him, but he teased her that he'd never live up to Ray in her mind. Granny would always smile and tell him that nobody was quite like Ray. It made me want to meet him."

"Your granny was right," Debbie said. "Raymond Zink is a class act and one of a kind. I think you'll enjoy him very much."

"Okay," Connie said. "We'll see you tomorrow."

Debbie said goodbye and ended the call. She looked at her two companions in complete shock—and then grinned. "Can you believe we finally found her?"

"It's a miracle," Kim said. "Now you just need to get Ray there to see her before it's too late."

"I know it'll be hard," Debbie said, "since we have so much to do here with the grand opening."

"It doesn't matter," Janet said. "This is a once-in-a-lifetime opportunity. We have to make this happen."

"I agree." Debbie smiled, excitement bubbling up. "Should we try to surprise Ray too?"

"It might be hard to get him into a car with us to go on a trip for two hours without telling him," Janet said. "But it's worth a try."

Debbie couldn't wait for the morning. She and Janet would go to Good Shepherd and try to convince Ray to go with them to Cameron, West Virginia.

He was about to learn what had happened to the love of his life, and Debbie and Janet would be there to witness it.

# CHAPTER SEVENTEEN

ebbie could hardly control her excitement and nerves the next day as they drove up to the Good Shepherd Retirement Center. She and Janet had met at the café that morning to pack a to-go lunch of sandwiches, chips, creamy cucumber salad, and cookies, and then they had left the café to head to the Good Shepherd.

It was now seven forty-five. If they left the assisted living home by eight, they could get to Eleanor's by ten. Debbie hoped Ray was awake and ready for the day.

"If he agrees to come without any questions," Debbie said to Janet as she pulled into a parking spot, "then we'll keep it a surprise. But if he isn't willing to go or is too suspicious, we'll have to tell him."

"I agree." Janet nodded. "Either way, we need to get him to Eleanor's."

"I'm sure if we walked in and said we found her, he'd start wheeling himself to Cameron."

"But think about how much more enjoyable it would be as a surprise," Janet said. "He'll be so excited."

"I hope so." Debbie turned off the car, and they both got out. "When he hears that she married someone else, I hope it doesn't devastate him."

"He had to come to that conclusion a long time ago." Janet closed her car door and came around the vehicle to join Debbie. "He had to realize it was a possibility if she was still alive."

"I just hope her health hasn't declined even more overnight." Debbie opened the front door and allowed Janet to precede her inside. "I want them to have a chance to talk."

"Same here."

They passed the women at the front desk, who smiled as they went by, but then one of them held up her hand.

"Ray's out in the courtyard, filling the bird feeders," she said as she pointed to her left. "You can find the door around the corner."

"Thank you." Debbie didn't bother to tell the woman that she knew her way around. She was just thankful that Ray was already awake.

The courtyard was a beautiful space with paved paths, benches, a water fountain, and lovely flower beds. It looked out from the back of the home with a view of a rolling yard rimmed with tall pine trees. Birds flitted about, landing on one of several bird feeders.

Ray was in his wheelchair, pulled up to a table, filling two of the feeders with seeds. He had a pleasant smile on his face, but when he glanced up and saw Debbie and Janet, his smile turned into a grin.

"Well, hello," he said. "I didn't expect to see you two so early in the morning."

"Hi, Ray," Debbie said, her pulse thumping with excitement.

"Hello," Janet echoed.

Ray handed one of the bird feeders to an employee, who returned it to its place on a hook a few feet away. Then he looked at Debbie and Janet. "What brings you here today?"

Debbie glanced at Janet, who nodded for her to continue.

"We have a surprise for you," Debbie said.

"Oh?" Ray finished filling the second feeder and then turned his full attention on Debbie and Janet. "What kind of surprise?"

"If we tell you," Janet said, "then it wouldn't be a surprise."

Ray chuckled. "I guess that's true."

"Do you like surprises?" Debbie asked.

For a second, he looked between the pair of them, and Debbie could see his mind working with all the possibilities. Finally, he said, "I love good surprises. Is this one good?"

"The very best."

Hope filled Ray's brown eyes, and he took a deep breath before he nodded.

Debbie suspected that he knew it had to do with Eleanor, but he didn't voice his guess. Instead, he said, "Where is the surprise?"

"In Cameron, West Virginia."

Ray looked down at his hands for a second, and Debbie could only imagine all the emotions flooding his mind and heart. He had to know this was about Eleanor—but what would it feel like to finally know the answer to a mystery that had plagued him for almost eighty years? Relief? Fear? Anger? Joy?

"Are you up for a ride, Ray?" Janet asked. "Would you be willing to come with us? We'll need to leave as soon as possible."

Without hesitation, Ray nodded. "I can be ready in ten minutes."

"That'll work," Debbie said. "Do you need help getting back to your room?"

"Would you mind?"

Debbie pushed Ray's wheelchair into the building and to his room. He didn't say a word, but he didn't need to. There was a nervous energy that emanated from him, communicating volumes.

They left him in his room and told him they'd be waiting in the entryway lobby.

Ten minutes later, he approached them in his wheelchair with his hair slicked down, wearing a nice pair of trousers, a dress shirt, and a navy blue cardigan. There was also a subtle scent of cologne.

In that moment, Debbie glimpsed a hint of Ray's youthful good looks and energy. He told the women at the front desk where he was going, and Debbie assured them that they'd get him home before bedtime.

Since Ray was able to stand and take a few steps on his own, they were able to help him into the front passenger seat and then fold up his wheelchair and put it into the trunk. Janet sat in the back seat, and Debbie got behind the wheel.

She paused for a second and smiled at him. "Are you ready?"

"Never more ready in my life."

Debbie put the address into her phone's GPS before pulling out of the parking lot.

"It's a two-hour drive," Debbie said to Ray. "Are you comfortable?"

"As comfortable as I'm going to get." Ray chuckled. He turned and looked at Janet. "Are you comfortable back there?"

"I'm great."

"Don't you two have a lot to do to get ready for your café opening?" Ray asked them.

"We've got almost everything done," Debbie said. "But we felt this was a more important way to spend our day."

Appreciation gleamed from Ray's eyes—but he still didn't ask them if they were going to see Eleanor. Debbie wasn't sure why. Perhaps he was afraid it was too good to be true. Maybe he thought they were going to a cemetery, or somewhere else that might answer some questions. Whatever he thought, he kept his guesses to himself.

Debbie glanced into the rearview mirror and smiled at Janet. She wanted to tell Ray, but she also wanted to see his reaction the moment he saw Eleanor again.

As they drove, Ray asked them about the café and about Debbie's house projects. She promised him she would take him there when it was all finished so he could see the changes she'd made. The conversation then shifted to other topics, but not once did they talk about the Salvation Army Canteen or the days that Ray worked at the depot. All three of them seemed to be avoiding the one topic that was most on their minds.

When the first sign for Cameron appeared on the road, Ray sat up a little straighter and Debbie's heart rate picked up speed. The GPS said they were only seventeen minutes away from the house.

Seventeen minutes—after Ray had waited eighty years to see Eleanor.

As Debbie followed the directions into Cameron, the three of them became very quiet.

The town was tiny, with less than a thousand people on the population sign. It was snuggled in a picturesque valley, with rolling hills and beautiful trees all around. They passed through a quaint covered bridge with a stream trickling beneath and pulled into the town. Many of the buildings were made of red brick and were several stories tall. The roads climbed the hills around downtown, crisscrossing back and forth, with houses and buildings nestled into the hillsides.

But it was the gas station on the corner that caught Debbie's eye. It was a modern station, and it had probably been updated several times since 1950, but the large sign out front was vintage and said JONES GASOLINE REFILLING STATION.

Was this the gas station Eleanor and Harrison had opened? Did the family still operate it today? It looked like a thriving business and well cared for.

Ray glanced at the gas station, but it could mean nothing to him, and Debbie didn't say a word.

They traveled two more blocks until they came to a pretty gray bungalow, similar to Debbie's house. It had a generous front porch, dormer windows on the upper floor, and cute shutters. A wheelchair ramp extended from the driveway to the front door.

Debbie pulled the car to a stop outside and checked the address one last time.

Ray looked at the house. "Are we here?"

"We are." Debbie put her hand over his. "Are you ready?"

He laid his other hand over hers. "If this is what I think it is, I've been ready for eighty years."

Debbie smiled and nodded before she squeezed his hand and got out of the car to bring him his wheelchair.

She hoped they weren't too late.

Sunshine sparkled down on the little bungalow as Debbie pushed Ray up the wheelchair ramp. Large, mature trees covered the property like a canopy, allowing the light to filter through, creating misshapen dots across the ground. They shifted and swayed as the wind moved the trees.

Ray was quiet as they came to the front steps. It was a comfortable home, with a swing hanging in one corner of the porch and potted ferns hanging between the eaves.

The front door opened, and a young woman in her midtwenties stood on the threshold. She had blond hair and brilliant blue eyes.

"Eleanor?" Ray breathed as he gazed at her.

"Hello," she said with a radiant smile. "I'm Connie, Eleanor's great-granddaughter. And you must be Raymond Zink."

He stared at her as if he were seeing a ghost, but then he blinked a few times and smiled. "You look just like Eleanor."

"Everyone's always telling me that." Her voice was warm and soothing, and she had a gentleness about her that instantly put Debbie at ease. "I think that's why I'm Granny's favorite." Her smile widened. "Although she tells all of her kids, grandkids, and great-grandkids that they're her favorite—and we all believe her." She extended her hand to Ray. "It's so nice to meet you, Mr. Zink. I've heard so many good things about you my whole life."

Ray took Connie's hand and looked up at her, tears in his eyes. "Is Eleanor here?" he whispered.

Connie clasped his hand in both of hers and nodded, though her face became serious. "She's on hospice care and fading fast, but she's awake right now. She seems to have a little more energy today."

"Hospice care?" Ray asked, swallowing hard.

"We're not sure how much time she has left." Connie's eyes also filled with tears. "But she'll be so happy to see you."

Debbie stepped forward, realizing she should explain a few things to Ray before they entered the house.

"We were able to find a journal entry from June Manley, dated 1950, that pointed us in this direction. We learned that Eleanor moved to Cameron that very year and started a gas station here." She paused, realizing that she should let Eleanor tell him the rest of her story. "You can ask her to tell you the rest."

Ray nodded. "May I see Eleanor now?"

"Come on in," Connie said as she opened the door wider. "She's in her bedroom."

Debbie pushed Ray into the house with Janet following them. It was cool inside and smelled like pine polish. Everything was neat and orderly. To the right was the dining room, and to the left of the main hall was the living room. Directly ahead of the front door was an open stairway and a door that led to what looked like a kitchen.

"This way," Connie said as she led them through the living room. A door at the back was closed, and she knocked lightly. "Granny?"

Connie entered the room and motioned for them to wait a moment, but Debbie could hear Connie speaking.

"Someone is here to see you," she said in a low, soothing voice. "I think you'll be very happy to see him, Granny."

"Who is it?" came a gentle, quiet voice.

Ray's eyes filled with tears, and he looked down at his hands. It was the first time he'd heard Eleanor's voice in eighty years, and it must be bittersweet. No doubt he had a hundred questions, but he waited patiently as their quiet words drifted toward them.

"I'll let you see for yourself," Connie said. She came to the door and opened it wider, indicating that Ray should enter.

Debbie pushed him into the room. It wasn't a large space, but it was bright and cheerful with two big windows allowing the dappled sunshine in. Vases of fresh-cut flowers were positioned throughout the room, and the walls were painted a pretty yellow with wide white trim.

Eleanor was in a hospital bed with the head raised. Though time had worn away her youth, she was still a beautiful woman. Her blue eyes looked sleepy at first, but they were soon bright with awareness as she looked from Janet to Debbie and then to Ray.

He stared at her, and she looked back at him—and in an instant, there was recognition in her eyes.

"Ray," she whispered. The one word was full of wonder, regret, and love. Without another word, she reached out a hand to him, and Debbie wheeled him the rest of the way so he could take her hand in both of his.

"Eleanor," he said, tears streaming down his cheeks. "My sweet, darling girl."

She tilted her head, and for a moment looked as young and pretty as she had in her pictures. "Girl?" She chuckled. "I haven't been a girl since the day you left Dennison."

Ray brought her hand to his lips and kissed it with such gentleness and reverence, Debbie's eyes filled with tears, and she took a step back to give them a little space.

"I never thought I'd see you again," Ray said to her. "I hoped and prayed, every day of my life, but I didn't know if God would allow it."

She ran her gaze over his face, taking him in with wonder. "I didn't think you'd ever want to see me again—not after what happened."

"I've looked for you and longed for you every day for the past eighty years, Eleanor. How could you ever think I would stop?"

She frowned. "What do you mean?"

"I've been looking for you since the day I returned from the war." He lowered his voice. "I never stopped loving you, Eleanor. There hasn't been any other woman in my life. Not one."

Eleanor's perplexity increased. "What about Mabel? Didn't you marry her?"

"Mabel?" It was Ray's turn to frown. "Mabel Thomas?" He shook his head. "She ran off with Sam Holman as soon as he came back from the war. They met at the canteen and wrote to each other for years. They bought a little farm and raised a family." He didn't take his eyes off her face. "I never married—always hoping and praying that one day I'd find you again."

"Oh, Ray." Eleanor's lips quivered, and she used her free hand to wipe her wrinkled cheek. "I'm so sorry—so very sorry for the pain I've caused you."

"You're forgiven," he said without hesitation. "It's forgotten. All that matters is that I've found you again."

Her quivering lips turned up in a smile. "I'm forgiven?"

"You've been forgiven from the start," he said. "But I'd really like to hear what happened after you left Dennison, if you'll tell me."

"First I'd like to tell you why I left Dennison," Eleanor said. "The man who took your job at the depot wasn't a very nice man, and he wouldn't leave me alone. He kept asking me to marry him, and it frightened me. When a friend asked me to go to Washington, DC with her and work for the Salvation Army, I agreed. But I made her promise not to tell anyone where we went."

"That's why I couldn't find anyone who knew," Ray said. "I'm so sorry I wasn't there to protect you."

Eleanor smiled at him. "I'd say he's lucky Uncle Sam was keeping you busy."

Debbie felt they were intruding on a private moment, so she said, "Maybe we should slip into the other room while you two talk?"

"No, no." Eleanor raised herself a little higher in the bed. "You brought Ray here for me, and I want you to hear the story too.

"When June and I got to Washington, that very first day, I became ill. Later, much later, I found out that it was polio. I came very close to death."

Debbie looked at Janet and saw her own feelings reflected on her friend's face. Tears stood in both their eyes.

"Thankfully, June and I were staying with a wonderful family that was able to nurse me back to health, but I didn't recover as we all hoped I would." She pointed to the empty wheelchair beside the bed. "I lost the use of my legs, and I didn't handle it very well. In my depression, I convinced myself that Ray would be better off without me. I thought it best for him to move on and find someone else. I was so ashamed."

"Ashamed?" Ray shook his head vehemently. "Why? It wasn't your fault."

"I don't know why. Maybe pride? I didn't think you'd want a wife who couldn't stand by your side."

"I would have taken you no matter what you looked like or what you could or could not do. You were my one true love, Eleanor, and nothing could have changed that."

"The years passed, and I figured you would have moved on," she continued. "Gotten married and had a family by then. I hoped you were happy. I met Harrison Jones in 1944. He had lost an arm in Germany, and he convinced me that neither of us were unlovable. It took a lot of time, but I finally agreed to be his wife." She paused and studied Ray's face. "I loved Harrison, but I also loved you, Ray. He knew that, and he was okay with it. He was a very good man, and God blessed us with four daughters."

"I bet they all looked like you," he said with a chuckle.

"They did. And each of them has given us granddaughters. Not a single boy among them." It was her turn to chuckle. "Much to Harrison's dismay. But he loved all his girls and took very good care of us."

Debbie glanced at Connie, who wiped away her tears. She smiled at Debbie.

"Harrison died a few years ago," Eleanor said, her voice starting to sound a bit weaker and tired.

"And you've been alone since then?" Ray asked.

"Not alone. I have my girls." She finally broke eye contact with Ray and looked at her great-granddaughter. "The family still runs the business, and they've taken care of me better than I deserve."

"Oh, Granny," Connie said and shook her head. "You deserve only the best."

"You've had a good life?" Ray asked Eleanor.

She looked back at him and nodded. "I have."

"Then that's all I could ask for," he said, his smile returning. "I'm content that you were happy, Eleanor. All my life, it's been my prayer for you. That no matter what happened, you were happy."

"Then God answered your prayer." She reached up and touched his cheek. "And what about you, Ray? Were you happy?"

"I've lived a good life," he said. "The only thing that would have made it better was having you by my side, but none of that matters anymore. I'm happy now."

They smiled at one another, and all the years seemed to melt away.

Ray let go of Eleanor's hand and reached into the pocket of his shirt. Slowly, he pulled out a beautiful diamond ring. The diamond was not large, but it still glinted in the sunshine coming through the window.

"I bought this for you when I first got to Europe and planned to give it to you the moment I stepped foot in Dennison."

"Oh, Ray." Tears filled Eleanor's eyes again.

"I've carried it with me every single day of my life, hoping and praying that God would allow me to finally give it to you." He took her hand again and gently laid the ring in her palm. "Today is that day—another answered prayer."

She wrapped her fingers around the ring and brought her hand up to her mouth, where she pressed her shaking fist against her lips, the tears flowing freely. When she had control of her emotions, she said, "Promise me you'll let yourself love again, Ray. If God gives you enough time, open your heart to love. You have so much to give."

Ray didn't speak for a moment, but finally he nodded. "I will."

Tears slipped down Eleanor's wrinkled cheeks, and she nodded as well. "I'm going home to the Lord very soon, Ray."

He studied her, his love and devotion shining from his face. "Then promise me that you'll wait for me there," he whispered to her. "And someday soon I'll join you."

Eleanor's eyes shone bright with hope and anticipation. "I promise," she whispered.

# CHAPTER EIGHTEEN

*C*onnie motioned for Debbie and Janet to follow her out of the room. As they walked out, all three ladies sniffled and wiped the tears from their cheeks. Connie grabbed a box of tissues in the living room and passed it around.

"For the rest of my life," she said, mopping the tears on her face, "I will not see anything as romantic as that moment."

Debbie was overcome with emotion, not only because of Ray and Eleanor's undying love for one another, but because she had never been given the chance to say one last goodbye to Reed. She couldn't help but wonder what she would have said had she been presented with the opportunity. Could she have been as eloquent as Eleanor and Ray?

"I'm thankful they got this final goodbye," Connie said as she balled up the tissue in her hand. "Eighty years is a long time, but I think it makes it that much sweeter."

With a deep, cleansing breath, Debbie nodded. "It's kind of amazing the series of events that transpired to bring us to this day. I was working in Cleveland and decided to give up my job there to move home to Dennison. I had always wanted to open a café, and Janet heard that the depot was willing to lease a space to us. We were able to get funding and a contractor all lined up to start renovating almost right away."

WHISTLE STOP CAFÉ MYSTERIES

"But it was the house that was the key to all of this," Janet reminded her.

"It was," Debbie agreed. "When Ray heard that I was coming back to Dennison, he contacted me to see if I wanted to buy his house. It's close enough to the depot that I can walk when I want, and it's just the right size for me. It's exactly what I would have chosen, had I been searching high and low. But I didn't have to search. It found me."

"And it was in the attic at Ray's that we found Eleanor's record," Janet added. "When Debbie brought it to Ray, he hadn't seen it in years and asked Debbie if she'd be willing to help him find Eleanor."

"So we started to look," Debbie concluded. "And the journey led us here."

"I'm so happy it did." Connie motioned for them to have a seat in the living room. "I honestly don't know how long Granny has to live. The rest of the family has been in and out the last few days to say goodbye, and the doctor has been by a couple of times. It's really odd that no one else is here right now. But Granny is ready. She's lived such a long and full life."

"You mentioned that Eleanor sang to you your whole life," Debbie said. "Did she use her gift in other ways?"

Connie smiled and nodded. "She sang in church almost every Sunday and was often invited to sing at the county fair and other events. Once she and Granddaddy had more money, he insisted she record all of her favorite songs, and he used to sell them at the fair when she sang."

"It sounds like your grandparents were wonderful together," Janet said.

"They were a great pair. Very loving and devoted to each other. He was her biggest fan. I wish you could have heard her sing."

"We've listened to the record she recorded for Ray in 1943." Debbie smiled. "She had a beautiful voice. She used to sing at the canteen dances during the war."

"And the canteen was at the depot where your café is now located?" Connie asked.

"That's right." Debbie had an idea. "It would be so neat to hear her voice at the depot again. I wonder if we could digitize her record and play it at the café."

Connie's eyes lit up. "Last year, my sister had all of her recordings digitized and copies made. Granny especially loved songs from the war years. The Andrews Sisters' were some of her favorites. I have a thumb drive with all of her songs. Would you like a copy?"

"Could we?" Debbie grinned. "We can play her songs for the grand opening, and then we could see if the museum director would like a copy, and perhaps she could incorporate one or two songs into the exhibits."

Tears filled Connie's eyes again, and she offered a tremulous smile. "I would love to know that Granny's voice will live on for others to enjoy. I think she might have some mementos from her days in Dennison too. A few pictures and some odds and ends from the canteen. Would you like those items as well? We have so many of Granny's things, I'd like to offer a few of them to you, if you think they are valuable."

"Yes," Debbie said. "We could create a shadow box to hang in the café. We're trying to decorate with World War II-era items. And if they have a personal connection to the depot, that's even better."

"Great. I know right where everything is. I'll be back in a bit." Connie left the living room and started up the hallway stairs.

Debbie smiled at Janet. "I'm so happy we came."

"So am I." Janet's face still showed remnants of her emotions. "And now that we know what happened to Eleanor, we can turn our entire attention toward the grand opening again. I think we should do a soft opening tomorrow night and invite some friends and family to stop by for supper. Might help us get out the jitters."

"That sounds like a great idea. As long as we have enough chairs."

"They should be there tomorrow."

"We can hope." But the chairs weren't the only thing on Debbie's mind. "Danica and Cori will be coming in tomorrow before supper. They can come to the café too."

"Great. I'm excited to meet them."

"I almost forgot. The carpet layers will be over in the morning. Once they're done, I'll be busy setting up the bedrooms, but that shouldn't take more than an hour or so. My parents had something come up, so Greg said he'd stop by to help me haul in some of the furniture. It's already in the basement, waiting in the corner of the main room. I can be at the café by midafternoon to help you prep for the soft opening."

"That's fine. If you need any help with your basement, don't forget to ask. I can probably sneak over to help."

"I think we'll be okay." Debbie hadn't seen Greg in a couple of days, and she was eager to tell him all about Ray's reunion with Eleanor. She found, more and more, that she wanted to share things with him. He was easy to talk to, and he had such a great outlook. He gave her a different perspective, which she appreciated.

Soon, Connie was back with a small box that she handed to Janet. "It's not much, but it's an important part of Granny's life. I love knowing she'll live on in Dennison through these things."

"We hope you'll have a chance to visit us one day," Debbie said. "It would be a pleasure to show you around the place that meant so much to her and Ray."

"I'd like that. Maybe I'll get my whole family to make the trip."

"And you'll let us know when Eleanor passes?" Debbie asked. "Maybe we'll be able to bring Ray back for the funeral."

"I will." Connie offered a sad smile. "I'm not eager for that day."

"No one ever is," Janet said, "but I'm so thankful that Eleanor has eternity with Christ to look forward to."

A radiant smile filled Connie's face, and she nodded. "Granny has been looking forward to meeting Jesus her whole life—and seeing Granddaddy again."

A soft, beautiful sound seeped from the bedroom, causing all three women to pause.

It was singing.

Connie stood and opened the bedroom door a crack, allowing Eleanor's voice to fill the room with a gentle, melodic tune. Her voice wasn't as strong and clear as it had once been, but it was still lovely, filled with a lifetime of love, loss, regret, and hope.

The three women stood spellbound as the notes and lyrics of *Don't Sit Under the Apple Tree* surrounded them. When Eleanor reached the hope-filled final line about marching home, Debbie pondered her own hope for eternity. Not only would she see Reed again, but she'd meet Jesus face-to-face, and that, to her, was the best hope of all.

For the first part of the car ride back to Dennison, Ray was very quiet. Neither Debbie nor Janet wanted to push him to talk before he was ready, so they respected his silence and said nothing.

But after a while, he turned to Debbie and simply said, "Thank you."

She smiled. "It was our pleasure, Ray."

"I didn't tell you this," he said, "but today is my birthday." He wiped tears from his cheeks. "It's so hard to believe that eighty years ago today I enlisted in the army, and that was the beginning of my losing Eleanor."

Debbie exchanged a wide-eyed look in the rearview mirror with Janet. His birthday?

"I don't know how to thank you for the best gift I've ever received. I honestly didn't think I'd ever get to see her again, this side of heaven." He looked straight ahead at the road. "I'm having a hard time understanding all the things I'm thinking and feeling right now."

"That's to be expected," Janet said from the back seat. "You've spent the majority of your life not knowing what happened to her. And now you do. I'm sure it'll take some time to come to terms with all of it."

"It was like I had this big, dark void in my mind and heart," Ray said. "A shadow of uncertainty. And, in the space of a few hours, the void is full of light, and I have pictures and information to fill all the uncertain parts. It's like my life is whole again—even if I didn't get to spend it with her. Now I know she was happy and fulfilled. She lived a good life."

"It was a very good life," Debbie agreed. "She was blessed."

"And that's all I really wanted," he assured them. "Of course I wanted her by my side. I loved her with all my heart. But I accepted a long time ago that it wasn't going to happen. I just prayed that wherever she was and whatever she was doing, she was filled with joy. And she was." He was quiet for a moment. "All these years, I pictured her as mine. She had promised me that she'd marry me and wait for me, so I felt possessive. While I sat there today, hearing her talk about Harrison and the family they created and the full life they lived, I realized that Eleanor didn't belong to me—and I didn't belong to her. And, somehow, that makes me feel free for the first time in my life."

Debbie reached over and gently squeezed his hand to acknowledge she understood how he felt.

"I'm ninety-eight years old." He chuckled as he shook his head. "Yet I feel kind of footloose and fancy free, as if I were eighteen again."

It was Debbie and Janet's turn to chuckle.

"What will you do with this new, fancy-free life?" Janet asked.

"I don't know." Ray smiled. "Maybe I'll ask someone out on a date."

Debbie couldn't help but think of Eileen and the sparkle she had in her eye when she played chess with Ray.

"Is there someone special you have in mind?" she asked.

"That's a good question." Ray looked out the passenger-side window, deep in thought. "I've never given myself permission to even consider the possibility. In my mind, I was committed to Eleanor, as if she were my wife. Isn't that silly?"

"You were in love and devoted," Janet said. "You were bound to a promise. I don't think it's silly. I think it's honorable and romantic."

Ray chuckled again. "Stubborn and bullheaded is more like it."

"Whatever it is," Debbie said, "it's part of your story, but your story isn't over. You have the choice to write whatever ending you want."

"I like that." Ray returned his attention to Debbie and Janet. "I still have an ending to write, and it can be whatever I'd like it to be."

"That's right," Debbie said. "All of us have the ability to write the stories we want in our lives. There may be twists and turns we don't see coming, but it's how we respond to those unexpected moments that truly defines who we are. I have faith that you'll respond to this twist in your story with as much dignity and honor as you've responded to all the others, Ray."

"I appreciate that." He looked lost in thought for a moment. "I think I used Eleanor's disappearance as an excuse to not take risks in love. It was easy to say that I couldn't pursue someone else because I was bound to a promise I made to her—but the truth is, I could have moved on years ago and possibly found happiness again. This has been a good reminder that sometimes risks are necessary for happiness."

It was Debbie's turn to look out the window and contemplate Ray's words. Was she using Reed's death as an excuse not to take risks in love again? Her mind immediately went to Greg and the attraction she felt toward him. It would be easy to pursue that relationship and see where it might take her, but the truth was, she was afraid. Not only of being hurt again but of being in love again. It was a vulnerable position, one that could either bring great happiness or intense sadness. She'd felt both emotions before, and the sadness had seemed to outweigh the happiness in the end. The one had been so fleeting, while the other seemed to hang over her head like a cloud for years.

And there was the added complication of Jaxon's feelings toward her. He didn't seem to like the idea of her and Greg becoming friends. Until he did, Debbie wouldn't even consider the possibility of following her heart.

Taking a deep breath, she returned her focus to the car ride and asked Ray more about Eleanor and their history together. She told him Connie was sending them a thumb drive full of her songs and they would share them with him, if he'd like. She also conveyed Connie's hope to come to Dennison one day with her family. Ray said he'd like to meet the rest of them, if they'd like to meet him.

It was good to see Ray coming to terms with the truth about Eleanor's disappearance. He seemed truly happy and relieved to finally know what had happened.

They stopped at a picnic area along the Ohio River near Wheeling and enjoyed the late lunch they'd packed. Ray praised the homemade bread that Janet had baked in the café, which prompted the ladies to invite him to come to the soft opening the following night. They told him that they planned to ask Harry and Eileen to come too, and Ray said it would be like a reunion.

When they finally got back to the Good Shepherd Retirement Center, Ray was laughing and telling stories with ease. He seemed to be filled with a newfound energy that belied his age and wheelchair.

Debbie pushed him through the open front door and into the lobby. She was surprised to see Eileen waiting there.

Eileen's face was full of apprehension as she studied Ray. "I heard that you went with Debbie and Janet to Cameron, West Virginia, today," she said to him. "And that it was a sudden trip. Is everything okay?"

Ray reached out to Eileen and took her hands in his. "Everything is wonderful," he said. "I saw Eleanor today."

Eileen gripped his hands, concern in her eyes.

"It's okay," Ray assured her. "Eleanor got married to a great guy, and they had a happy, full life together. I'll tell you all about it tonight, over a game of chess."

A glint of teasing filled Eileen's eyes. "You sure you want to risk losing to me again?"

"I might lose again," he conceded. "But there's also a chance I might win. And as long as there's a chance, I'll try again and again and again."

Eileen smiled and put her hand on Ray's cheek. "Maybe, one of these times, I'll let you win."

Ray winked at her. "Don't give in too soon. The thrill of the game is why we play, after all."

Debbie and Janet laughed and said their goodbyes.

As they pulled away from the assisted living home, Debbie considered Ray's words. *I might lose again, but there's also a chance I might win. And as long as there's a chance, I'll try again and again and again.*

She felt the same way.

# CHAPTER NINETEEN

On Friday morning, Debbie opened her eyes and found she still had a smile on her face. She stretched out in bed and let the memories from the day before blanket her in a cocoon of happiness. She and Janet had helped Ray find his Eleanor, and though they didn't get the happily-ever-after ending that she would have liked, they still found peace and closure.

She couldn't help but wonder what Ray was thinking about as he woke up this morning. It would be the first time in almost eighty years that he would wake up without any questions or doubts in his mind about the woman who had disappeared so long ago.

Debbie's alarm went off on her phone, and she reached over to turn it off. The carpet layers were going to be coming in about an hour, and she still had a few things to get ready before they could install it. She wanted to vacuum the cement floors in each room one more time, just to make sure there was no loose debris from the construction phase.

She jumped out of bed, quickly got dressed, and made herself some breakfast before sitting down to do her morning devotions. She had several books she liked to read from, but one was a daily devotion with a short story and prayer that included a few Bible verses to look up. It was her favorite and a great way to start each day.

At nine o'clock, she started to keep an eye out for the carpet layers as she vacuumed in the basement. The windows in the bedrooms looked out at the driveway, and that was where she had told the carpet layers to park, since it would be the easiest, shortest access to the basement from there.

When she was done in the basement, she went back upstairs and vacuumed the rugs in the entryway and the living room. Her house was clean, so she didn't have a lot of work to prepare for her guests. She would wipe down the guest bathroom in the basement and do a load of laundry, but other than that, she didn't have a lot to occupy her time until the carpet was laid and it was time to bring in the furniture. Then she'd be off to the café until her friends arrived later that afternoon.

Debbie glanced out the window again, but still no carpet layers, which meant they were late. Her phone rang, so she pulled it out of her back pocket and saw that it was Janet calling.

"Hey," Janet said. "How does the carpet look?"

"I don't know. It's not here yet."

"Tradespeople are often late. I'm sure they'll be there soon."

"Are the chairs there yet?"

Janet paused. "No, but he said they'd be here before the grand opening."

"That only leaves today—and with our soft opening tonight, we need those chairs."

"I'll call him again. Some better news for you is that Dale is working in the restroom. The drain piece came, and he's installing it. All he has to do is finish up the trim today, and it'll be ready for use."

"That is good news." Debbie looked outside again. "Thank you for letting me know."

"I've texted and called almost everyone on our list, inviting them for supper at the café tonight, and it sounds like most people can make it." There was a smile in Janet's voice. "But I didn't call Greg. I figured you could ask him when he stops by your place today—that is, if you still want him to come."

"Of course. I'd love to have him and his boys there with us."

"Great. I'll leave his invitation up to you, then."

Debbie thought she heard something and looked out at the driveway, but no one was there.

"I'll see you later," Janet said. "I have some prepping to do for tonight's meal."

"Bye." Debbie ended the call and walked to the front porch, where she stood for a few minutes, watching for the carpet truck.

Where was it?

Her phone rang again, and this time it was Greg.

"Hey," he said. "Are the carpet layers having any trouble with your basement steps? I was thinking about how hard it might be to get a roll of carpet down them."

"They're not here yet," Debbie said as she looked at the clock in her entryway. "They're almost an hour late."

"Hmm. That doesn't sound like Fred. He's usually punctual. Maybe something came up. I'll give him a call and get back to you."

"Thanks."

"Hold tight." Greg ended the call, and Debbie stood for a moment, wondering what to do with herself. She had a ton of work ahead of her, but each chore was dependent on the one before it. If the carpet didn't get laid, she couldn't get the rooms settled, and if she couldn't get the rooms settled, she couldn't get to the café.

She decided to start prepping the egg bake for tomorrow's breakfast. She had planned to do it later that evening, but it could sit in the fridge for a few extra hours, and it would give her more time with her friends before bed.

As she worked on assembling the ingredients, her phone rang again, and it was Greg.

"Hello," she said with a smile in her voice, hoping he had good news.

"Hey." His voice didn't sound as chipper as it had before. "I talked to Fred, and there was a mix-up with his schedule." He sighed. "He and his crew are out of town today putting in a massive installation. He has you on his schedule for next Friday."

Debbie sat on the kitchen stool near her counter. "Next Friday?"

"I'm sorry, Debbie. I have no idea how this happened."

"What will I do? Danica and Cori are coming tonight—and the floor is awful." There was spilled paint and stains all over the place from all the construction mess. "Not to mention it's cold on the feet." She felt like crying—which was silly, given the situation. There were so many other things that could be wrong, yet she had put a lot of money and effort into those rooms, and she wanted them to be nice for her friends.

Greg was quiet for a moment, and then he said, "I have an idea. I'll be over there in about thirty minutes. Don't worry, okay?"

What other choice did she have? She tried not to sound too dejected as she said, "Okay."

After ending the call, Debbie sat for a few minutes on her stool, trying to keep her emotions at bay. It was silly to be so upset. Danica and Cori would understand. But it was still disappointing.

She finished getting the egg bake ready and covered it with plastic wrap before putting it into her refrigerator.

Thirty minutes later, Greg pulled into her driveway in his pickup truck—backward.

Debbie glanced out and saw that the bed of his truck was full of area rugs.

She frowned as she opened the kitchen door, wondering what he was doing.

Jaxon, Julian, and Hammer jumped out of the truck, and Julian waved hello at her, while Jaxon barely acknowledged her.

"What's this?" Debbie asked as Greg came around to the truck bed.

"Plan B," he said with a big smile. "We're going to cover the floors with rugs until the carpet can come next week. This way, your friends don't have to look at the ugly floors, and their feet will stay warm."

"Where did you get all of them?" Debbie inspected the rugs and found they were made from beautiful, high-quality materials, and many of them had lovely patterns that would match her decor.

"I know Fred felt bad, so I called him back and asked if I could borrow the display rugs from his showroom. He didn't hesitate, so the boys and I ran over there and took all the rugs we could find that were close to the color you'd ordered. You can keep the ones you choose until Fred comes to lay your carpet next Friday. And he won't charge you an installation fee. He said it's on him."

Debbie pressed her lips together and shook her head, again trying not to cry. "You did all this for me?"

"Hey." He put his arm around her shoulder and tried to get her to smile. "The last thing I want is a dissatisfied customer. I take my job seriously—and I promised you we'd have those rooms looking sharp for your friends' arrival, didn't I?"

His arm felt strong and protective before he pulled away. "Thank you," she said, wiping her cheeks to get rid of the tears. "I can't thank you enough."

He smiled as he motioned for the boys to start hauling the rugs into the house. "We won't need all of them," he said to Debbie, "but we'll take them in and see which ones fit the best. How does that sound?"

"Perfect."

"And then the boys and I will help you move the furniture into the bedrooms and get them set up. Will that be okay?"

"Thank you, Greg," Debbie said again. "This means a lot to me."

He smiled at her as the boys started to carry the rugs into the house.

"What are friends for?" he asked, his eyes softening. "And, though I go to great lengths to keep my customers satisfied, I go even further for friends."

She wanted to hug him, right then and there, but Jaxon was frowning, and Debbie wasn't sure if Greg would be uncomfortable with her show of affection.

"I appreciate that," she said instead. "And to show you how much, I'd like you and the boys to join us tonight at the café for a soft opening. Janet and I will be serving supper to our friends and family—and since we're such good friends, I'd love for you to be there."

It was Greg's turn to smile as he nodded. "We'll be there."

"Great."

Debbie helped them carry the rugs to the basement, and then she and Greg chose the perfect ones to fit in the rooms.

After they settled on the right ones, they brought in the beds, dressers, and chairs that Debbie had chosen for each room. Then Greg and the boys put together the shelves and hanging rods she'd ordered last week while she made the beds. The soft comforters, combined with the beautiful, plush rugs, gave each room a warm, homey glow. Lamps added a touch of light, and Debbie hung some of her favorite pictures on the walls. She'd purchased fresh-cut flowers and set a vase in each room to complete the look.

When they were done, well before Debbie had thought they would be, she and Greg stood back and admired their work. The boys had gone up to the kitchen to enjoy some lemonade and cookies.

"What do you think?" Greg asked her.

"I love it," Debbie said with a satisfied smile.

"You think your friends will be comfortable here?"

"I think they're going to have a great weekend—and so am I." She turned her gaze from the room to look at Greg. "I appreciate your efforts to go above and beyond your job for me."

He met her gaze, and there was something deep and meaningful in his eyes. "I would do it over and over again for you, Debbie. All you have to do is ask."

She felt something stir to life in her heart—a place inside her that had fallen asleep when Reed died. It both exhilarated and frightened her, but she heard the message from him. All she had to do was ask.

And, right now, she wasn't ready to ask.

Maybe one day. But not yet.

A soft rain had begun to fall that afternoon as Debbie and Janet made last-minute plans for the soft opening at the café. Janet had finished all her cookies and baking for the big grand opening the following day and had all the supplies on hand for supper that night. She would serve baked chicken, mashed potatoes, gravy, corn, and dinner rolls. It was a meal she planned to rotate as a blue-plate special in the weeks and months ahead and thought it would be a great choice to serve their guests.

Debbie called the upholsterer, and he said he would have the chairs delivered before five. She made him promise, but she still was apprehensive. She had to leave the café at three, since her friends were coming at four, and then she wanted to get back to the café to help set up the chairs.

"Dale?" Debbie called as she approached the restroom where she'd been listening to him work all afternoon. "How is it going in here?"

"Great." He grinned at her as he tacked a piece of trim above the door. "I'm just about to put the last piece of trim on, and then I'll put wood putty in all the holes and seams and be out of your way."

She admired his work and was pleased to see that everything looked in great shape. She even turned on the water faucet to make sure the drain worked.

"Can you stay for supper tonight?" she asked him. "We're doing a soft opening, and it wouldn't be right to serve it without you."

"I'd be honored." He nodded. "I've been smelling that delicious aroma coming out of the kitchen all day. I was hoping to try some of Janet's cooking."

"We'll plan to serve the meal at six. Be sure to call your family and get them here too." As long as the chairs were there. If not, their guests would be sitting on the floor picnic-style.

"Great. I'll work extra hard to get this done in time."

"Perfect."

Debbie glanced at the clock on her phone and saw that it was close to three. She wanted to get home and shower before Danica and Cori arrived.

For some reason, her pulse picked up speed at the thought of her friends' arrival. What would they think when they pulled into Dennison? The population was just over two thousand—about a thousand times smaller than Cleveland. Would they think she was foolish for giving up her well-paying job to risk it all on a small café, in a small town?

She pushed aside her misgivings and poked her head into the kitchen, where Janet was happily chopping potatoes to prepare them for boiling.

"I'm heading home to shower and wait for Danica and Cori. Is there anything else I can help with before I leave?"

"Not a thing," Janet said with a grin. "I've got it all under control. Tiffany is going to be here soon to help me. I know you're eager to welcome your friends to town, so don't worry about a thing here."

"I'll be back as soon as possible."

"Take your time, Debbie. I'm perfectly content right here, doing what I love most in the world."

Debbie returned Janet's smile. "Thank you."

"You're welcome."

"I mean for everything. I couldn't have done this without you."

Janet paused and set her potato down. She gave Debbie a big hug. "And I couldn't have done this without you either. We make a great team." She pulled away and then shooed Debbie out of the kitchen. "Go on and have fun. You've worked hard to enjoy this weekend. I'll see you later."

Debbie left the café with mixed emotions. She was so thankful for Janet's competency and willingness to help, but she felt a little guilty for leaving her.

It didn't matter how she felt, though, because her guests were already on their way. Danica had texted when they left Cleveland about forty minutes ago, which meant they would be at her house in less than an hour.

She jumped into her car and drove home. There, she took a quick shower, got dressed in a fresh outfit, touched up her makeup, and then made sure everything was in place for her guests.

A few minutes before four, a car pulled into the driveway, and she heard the horn honk.

Debbie grinned. She'd missed her friends more than she realized.

She'd known Cori the longest, having met her when she took the job in Cleveland. Danica had joined the team about five years later, and they'd all gotten along from the start. Through the years, they'd not only worked together but had bonded over the ups and downs of life.

Debbie opened the kitchen door and stepped out to greet them.

"Welcome to Dennison!" she said with a big smile.

Danica was tall, with dark hair and brown eyes. She took in the neighborhood, the house, and then Debbie with a grand, sweeping glance. "This is so charming," she said with a bit of awe. "Like coming home to Mayberry."

Cori stepped out of the car next. She was shorter, with tight, curly hair and a freckled complexion. She smiled too. "I love it, Debbie. This is amazing. And you look great. You're glowing!"

Debbie gave each of them a big hug. "I'm so happy you came all this way."

"It was such a nice drive," Danica said. "Barely any traffic once we got out of Cleveland."

"And such pretty countryside," Cori added. "I think you'll have to put out the welcome mat often. This might become my weekend retreat."

"You're always welcome." Debbie helped them with their bags and showed them into the house through the front door, because she loved the beauty of her entryway.

"This is so pretty," Danica said as she oohed and aahed over the woodwork, the lead-glass windows, and the hardwood floors. "Can you imagine how expensive this house would be in the city?"

Debbie didn't want to tell them what a steal she'd gotten on the house, knowing she was paying less per month on her mortgage than they did on monthly rent for apartments one-tenth the size—not to mention she had a garage and yard.

"I have guest rooms in the basement for you," Debbie said, feeling a little apprehension. "I had them recently remodeled—but the carpet didn't get laid this morning like it was supposed to."

"That's okay," Cori said.

Debbie led them down the steps and into the basement.

"Wow," Danica said as they entered the first room. "I don't know why I thought we were coming to help you get settled this weekend. You've got it all done."

"Same here," Cori added. "I didn't realize we were going to be pampered."

"Pampered?" Debbie laughed. "I might put you to work in the café."

"That's fine by me." Danica set her bag on the bed. "I truly didn't think you'd have the café *and* your house ready so soon. Like I said, I thought we would be helping you."

"What gave you that idea?" Debbie asked.

"The fact that you've only been here a few weeks," Cori said. "You've done so much work, Debbie. This is amazing." She looked at the rugs. "And I love the look in here. I wouldn't change a thing."

"You must have had a lot of help," Danica added.

Debbie thought about all the work Greg had done to help her, and she smiled. "I did. Greg was over—"

"Greg?" Cori set down her own bag and gave Debbie an eager expression. "Who is Greg?"

"A friend," Debbie said, though her cheeks grew warm at the looks her friends gave her. It was hard to hide the truth from them. "He's just a friend," she insisted. "He's the one who brought over the rugs."

"Will we meet this Greg?" Danica asked.

"Yes. Tonight, at the café."

Danica and Cori looked at each other and smiled. Debbie could see that they were both pleased—and not just about Greg but about everything.

When Cori looked back at Debbie, her expression softened. "You look good, Deb. Really, really good. I can see this move was exactly what you needed."

"It *was* exactly what I needed," she agreed. "And though I miss you guys and parts of my life in Cleveland, I don't regret the move for a moment."

"You shouldn't." Danica gave her another hug. "I've been hoping and praying you're happy."

Debbie looked from her friends to the room and down at the rugs Greg had brought. She thought about helping Ray find Eleanor and all the connections she'd already made with Harry, Kim, Eileen, and the others, and knew that she was where she belonged.

"Come on," she said, pushing aside her thoughts to focus on her friends. "I want to take you to the café and introduce you to Janet. We're going to host a soft opening tonight with a bunch of friends, and if you really want to help, there will be plenty to do."

"Sign me up," Danica said. "I can't wait."

Debbie let them get their things settled, and then she had them pile into her car so she could take them to the café. Instead of taking the direct route, she drove them through the tree-lined streets and avenues of Dennison. She showed them where she'd gone to school, where she had played on the playground as a child, where her favorite pizza place was, and even where she'd had her first kiss in McCluskey Park, near Little Stillwater Creek.

When she noticed it was almost five, she took them to the café.

The aromas wafting out of the kitchen were mouthwatering.

It was fun to see the café through Danica's and Cori's eyes, especially when they praised it so highly.

"I know I keep saying this, but Dennison is so charming," Cori said. "I love it."

"It's so quintessential small town. It makes me want to come here every day," Danica added.

Janet must have heard them, because she came out of the kitchen, wiping her hands on a dish towel. She wore one of her fun T-shirts, the one that said, Keep Calm and Bake On, and she had a huge smile on her face.

"Cori and Danica," Debbie said, "this is my good friend and business partner, Janet."

The women shook hands, and Danica said, "We've heard so much about you."

"I can say the same." Janet smiled. "Welcome to Dennison."

"We're happy to be here," Cori said. "And we're ready to work. What can we do to be helpful?"

Janet had jobs for all of them. After introducing them to Tiffany, she gave each of them an apron and put them to work.

As Debbie laughed with her friends, watching her old life connect to her new one, she realized she had never felt more peaceful or sure of herself than she did in that moment.

Now, if only the chairs would get there, everything would be perfect.

# CHAPTER TWENTY

It was quarter to six, and Debbie poked her head out the café door, apprehension winding its way up her throat. "Where are those chairs?" she asked whoever was listening to her.

"When were they supposed to get here?" Cori asked as she set salt and pepper shakers on the tables.

"By five." Debbie came back into the café and shook her head. "Where is everyone going to sit?"

"We'll make do," Danica promised.

"I'm not just worried about today," Debbie said. "I'm thinking about tomorrow too."

"Do you know of anyone who has folding chairs you could borrow?" Danica asked.

"I suppose the church does—but it's the principle of the matter." Debbie had found that being in business for herself was more frustrating than she had anticipated. "We paid to have the chairs reupholstered, and we were guaranteed that they'd be delivered on time. That's what we're paying for."

Debbie pulled out her phone to call the company again, but no one answered. She locked her phone and stuffed it into her back pocket, trying to remain calm.

The bell over the door rang, and Harry entered the café, his ever-present companion at his side.

"We're early," he said. "I hope that's okay."

"Come on in, Harry," Debbie said as she introduced him to Danica and Cori. "Have a seat at the counter. As you can see, we don't have any chairs yet."

"Don't mind if I do."

Debbie went to the coffeepot and filled a mug for him.

"I heard Ray and Eileen are coming over," Harry said with a grin. "It's been a while since I've seen that pair."

"They should be here any moment," Debbie said. "Kim went to pick them up."

Ian arrived next, followed soon after by Debbie's mom and dad. Debbie made the introductions and handed out coffee and beverages as people began to visit and mingle.

Janet and Tiffany came out of the kitchen to greet their guests, and no one seemed to notice that there were no chairs at the tables.

Soon Greg arrived with his boys. He walked in and immediately sought Debbie's gaze. When he caught it, he offered her a big smile.

"Congratulations," he said, producing a bouquet of fresh-cut flowers.

Debbie was taken aback, not expecting such a gesture. Her cheeks warmed as she took them. "Thank you so much, Greg."

"I wish you all the best with your dreams, Debbie. And, being a small-business owner myself, I also wish you all the patience, good humor, and determination you can muster."

She laughed and then noticed that Danica and Cori had taken a keen interest in this new arrival.

"Come meet my friends," she said to him.

"I'd like to."

As Debbie introduced Danica and Cori to Greg, the door opened again and Eileen walked in, followed by Kim, who pushed Ray in his wheelchair.

Ray's face shone as he looked around the café with curiosity and awe. Harry got off his stool to shake his old friend's hand. Eileen greeted Harry with warmth. Kim knew several people in the room and was soon absorbed in a conversation as Janet's parents arrived next.

The room filled up quickly, and the meal was almost ready to be served—but there was nowhere for the guests to sit. The counter would only hold six of them.

When the door opened again, Debbie turned to see a stranger standing there.

She walked over to him. "We're not open to the public yet."

"I'm here with some chairs," the young man said. "I have forty chairs to deliver."

Greg must have heard, because he joined Debbie. "Do you need help bringing them in?"

"That'd be great," the man said.

Greg called for his sons, drawing the attention of everyone else in the room.

Soon there was a stream of people going in and out, hauling in the chairs.

Debbie couldn't hide her relief. They finally had their chairs, and they matched the decor perfectly.

"Thank you," Debbie said to the delivery man. She signed the invoice he handed her.

"Sorry they were late. I took a wrong turn and got lost."

Debbie couldn't blame him for that, so she thanked him again and closed the door behind him when he left.

She walked over to Janet, who was admiring the gathered crowd.

"Are we ready?" Debbie asked her.

"I think we are. The food is ready to be plated and served."

Debbie met Janet's gaze. "I mean, are we ready for this next big adventure?"

A smile spread across Janet's face, and she nodded. "I've been looking forward to it for a long time."

"Let's have a prayer before we eat," Debbie said. "I don't want to do anything without God at the forefront."

"That's a great idea," Janet said. "It seems only right that our soft opening should start with Him in mind."

"Can I have everyone's attention?" Debbie called out to the room.

It took a little while, but the room quieted, and everyone turned to look at Debbie and Janet.

Debbie smiled at their friends and family. "Janet and I would like to take this opportunity to thank each and every one of you for being here tonight. We invited you because every one of you has played a part in helping us achieve this dream."

There were smiles all around.

"We've known some of you for many years," Janet continued, "and some of you we've only recently met. Either way, we thank you, from the bottom of our hearts, for supporting our dream to open the Whistle Stop Café."

The room erupted with applause, causing Debbie's emotions to well up again. She'd cried quite enough in the past couple of days and was ready to just smile.

Part of her wished Reed were here. Each time she made a big life change, she remembered him, wondering what he would have thought about her choices. Would he be proud of her for stepping out in faith and moving back to Dennison to open the Whistle Stop Café? She liked to think so.

"Now," Debbie said, pushing aside her thoughts to focus on this moment, "I'd like to say a prayer before we ask you to find a seat so we can begin serving the meal. If you'd bow your heads with me, I'll begin."

Everyone bowed their heads, and the room quieted.

"Lord," Debbie prayed, "we thank You for bringing all of us here today. We thank You for Your blessings and provisions and for Your calling in each of our lives. We dedicate and commit this business to You today and every day, and we ask that You would bless each meal we serve here. In Your name we pray. Amen."

Several amens echoed throughout the room before people lifted their heads again.

"If you'd like to find a seat," Debbie said, "we'll start the meal."

There were plenty of chairs for everyone now, and they each took a seat. Ray sat at a table with Eileen, Harry, and Kim. Debbie's and Janet's parents sat together, and Dale sat with his wife and two grandkids. Tiffany, Julian, and Jaxon sat at the counter, and Greg sat at a table with Ian, while Danica and Cori insisted that they help Debbie and Janet prep the dinner plates and serve them to their guests.

Laughter and conversation soon filled the café, echoing off the yellow walls. As Debbie served the meal, refilled beverages, and, eventually, took her own plate to sit down and sample the food, she listened to the sound of those enjoying themselves and realized that it was exactly what she'd been hoping to hear since the day she decided to open the Whistle Stop Café.

Tomorrow was going to be another big day—the biggest—and this soft opening had given her the confidence she needed to face it with excitement.

It was the day Debbie had been waiting for. Outside, the morning was crisp and brand-new. Sunshine poured into her bedroom, a bird sang in a nearby tree, and everything looked fresh.

She had awakened before her alarm clock rang again, so she just lay in bed for a few minutes and soaked up the moment. She had stayed up later than she had planned the night before with Cori and Danica as they had visited in her living room. Not only had they reminisced about the years Debbie lived and worked in Cleveland, but they had discussed all the new things Debbie was doing in Dennison. They wanted to know more about Greg and more about Debbie's search to find Eleanor. They asked her about her church, the house, and all sorts of things.

In turn, Debbie chatted with them about their own personal lives and the things that concerned them.

Now, as Debbie lay in bed, thinking about last night and contemplating today, she thought she would feel tired. But the reverse was true. She was energized and excited to face the day.

She turned off the alarm before it sounded and slipped out of bed. The grand opening would start at ten this morning and end at two. They were closed on Sundays, which would give Debbie more time to spend with her guests, and then on Monday morning, they would begin their permanent schedule, opening at seven.

It felt right and good to start the day in prayer and thanksgiving. She usually did her devotions in the kitchen, but today, she knelt beside her bed to offer her thanks to God. It was good to release the energy she felt building inside her and to pour out all her praise, along with her requests, in the privacy of her bedroom.

When she was done, she got dressed and went into the kitchen to put the egg bake into the oven. About ten minutes later Danica joined her, and then Cori soon after.

"Mmm," Cori said. "Something smells good."

"Breakfast," Debbie said. "We'll eat and then head over to the café to get ready for the grand opening."

"Will Greg be there again?" Danica asked with a wink and a smile.

"I don't know." Debbie knew her friends were only teasing, but there was a part of her that didn't want to be teased about Greg. She wanted to hold her thoughts and feelings about him close, not letting anyone else either encourage or discourage her.

"I can tell he likes you," Danica said.

"That's good, because I like him too. And, I like Harry and Eileen and Ray—"

"You know what I mean, Deb," Danica said.

"I do know what you mean," Debbie conceded, "but I need more time. We're only just getting to know each other."

Danica seemed to accept her response, and they got busy preparing their breakfast.

Soon they were back in the car and on their way to the café.

Janet's car was already parked outside, so they were able to enter the building without Debbie's key.

It smelled like coffee and sweet rolls. Since they wouldn't be fully open and operational until Monday, they had decided to offer a reduced menu for their first day in business. Already, the bakery case was full of cinnamon and caramel rolls, muffins, and cookies. On the board, Janet had written the blue-plate special, which was the only meal they'd be serving for the opening. It was chicken and dumplings, along with the soup of the day, which was beef vegetable.

Danica and Cori entered the café as if they'd been working as waitresses their whole lives. They found their aprons and began to clean the salt and pepper shakers and refill the napkin dispensers.

Debbie joined Janet in the kitchen. "Good morning," she said.

"Oh! Good morning. Happy grand-opening day."

Debbie grinned. "The same to you."

"I'm just about ready in here."

"And we'll be ready out there soon."

"Sounds good." Janet had to stir something in a pot and then took a batch of cinnamon rolls out of the oven. She moved with such grace and elegance in the kitchen, Debbie had no question as to whether or not Janet was made for this kind of work.

It was soon ten o'clock, and the very first customer through the door was Harry, with Crosby nearby.

"Congratulations," Harry said as he came in and found his seat at the counter. "I'll have some coffee, if you don't mind. And one of those cinnamon rolls."

"Coming right up," Debbie said with a smile. She already knew she would love being in the front of the café, visiting with customers, serving tables, and running the daily operations.

Within minutes, people began to pour in. Many of them were curiosity seekers, having heard that the café was opening in the old depot and saying how they wanted to come in to see what the two women had done to the place.

Debbie had brought in her computer and some speakers and played Eleanor's songs at a gentle volume. It gave the café a nostalgic feel, coupled with the posters on the wall and the history of the building.

Almost everyone who came in was there to eat, so Danica and Cori helped Debbie serve the tables. There were so many people that guests had to wait for a table to open, and the cinnamon rolls and caramel rolls ran out before lunchtime. After that, the chicken and dumplings became the big hit.

Janet was busy in the kitchen, poking her head out from time to time to say hello and check on everyone. She visited with several customers to ask what they thought of the food, hoping to make improvements where needed.

Many of the visitors were familiar to Debbie, but the majority of them were not. They came not just from Dennison but also from their surrounding communities. Kim popped in for a moment to say that the museum had seen a huge bump in visitors as well, thanks to the café.

There were people from church, old neighbors, friends from school, and various family members. Greg and his boys stopped in for lunch, offering another round of congratulations.

Debbie's cheeks hurt from smiling, and her forearm was getting a workout from pouring coffee. She loved hearing everyone's comments about the café and their stories about the depot. A few people remembered the canteen and even commented on the music they were playing. Debbie was able to tell them it was Eleanor O'Reilly, though no one remembered her except Harry. But it still felt like Eleanor was there with them, just as she had been in 1943, serving coffee and smiles, making people feel welcome and at home.

The customers slowly trickled down until it was two o'clock and the last group left the café. Debbie turned the sign to Closed and locked the door.

Danica and Cori were eating a late lunch at the counter, and Janet was in the kitchen, cleaning.

Debbie let out a contented sigh as she felt her phone vibrate in her back pocket.

She pulled it out and saw Ray's name pop up on the screen.

"Hello, Ray."

"Hello, Debbie." His voice was quiet. "How did the grand opening go?"

"It was wonderful. I haven't sat down in hours."

"I'm happy to hear that, and I'm sorry I couldn't be there. My arthritis is acting up today."

"It's okay. We were happy to have you last night and look forward to seeing you here again soon."

"I waited to call you until after two, since I knew the grand opening ended then. I would have waited longer, but I thought you'd like to know."

Something caught in Debbie's spirit, and she held her breath.

"Connie phoned me earlier this morning to let me know that Eleanor passed away in her sleep last night, peacefully."

Debbie closed her eyes briefly. "I'm so sorry to hear that, Ray."

"I am too." He paused. "But I'm happy that I was able to say goodbye and that I know this time she'll be waiting for me when I get home."

Debbie smiled. "I'm so thankful for that assurance."

"Me too. And I want to say thank you, again, for finding her for me. I'm grateful to you."

"It was my pleasure, Ray. If there's ever anything else you need help with, you let me know."

"And the same to you. I plan to be here for a lot longer, God willing, and I'd like to still feel useful. You come and visit often, and let me know if I can be of help."

"I will."

"Goodbye."

"Goodbye, Ray."

Debbie slipped her phone into her pocket as Janet exited the kitchen. She met Debbie's gaze, and Janet must have seen the look on her face.

"Is everything okay?" Janet asked.

"Eleanor passed away in her sleep last night."

Janet's smile fell. "Isn't that how we all hope to go? Live a long, happy life and then pass away in our sleep?"

Debbie smiled. "I suppose you're right."

A train whistle blew in the distance and soon barreled past the depot, reminding Debbie of all the troop trains that had passed through the depot during the war. She thought about Ray, Eleanor, Eileen, Harry, and the others who were such an important part of that history.

And now she and Janet were part of the history of the Dennison depot, forever ingrained in the building and its story.

She liked thinking about it that way—and liked knowing that it was just the beginning of their story.

Dear Reader,

The WWII era has always been fascinating to me, especially the home-front efforts of the American people. When I was in high school, my uncle taught a WWII class to our homeschool co-op. Early on, we were tasked with choosing a topic about the war. I was the only female in the group and had very little interest in choosing a battle to report on as all my classmates were doing. When I talked to my uncle about this, he said that I should research the home front. One of my classmates scoffed and said that the home front had nothing to do with the war. My uncle was quick to correct him. He said that the work done by those on the home front was vital in winning the war. The soldiers couldn't have done it without them. I never forgot his remarks or all the amazing things I learned about the men and women who served on American soil between 1941 and 1945. One of those efforts was the canteens that popped up at railroad depots throughout the country to feed, encourage, and support the boys going to war.

It was a pleasure to return to the home front in *Under the Apple Tree* and learn more about the Salvation Army Canteen at the

Dennison Depot. I truly hope I get to visit there in person one day, but until then, I look forward to reading all the other books in the Whistle Stop Café series. I hope you'll join me.

Enjoy!

Signed,

Gabrielle Meyer

# ABOUT the AUTHOR

Gabrielle Meyer lives in central Minnesota on the banks of the upper Mississippi River with her husband and four children. As an employee of the Minnesota Historical Society, she fell in love with the rich history of her state and enjoys writing fictional stories inspired by real people, places, and events. Gabrielle has over thirty novels in print, including bestselling historical, contemporary, and cozy mysteries.

# GLIMPSE of the PAST

The song "Don't Sit Under the Apple Tree (With Anyone Else but Me)" was a featured song in the story, *Under the Apple Tree*. It was made famous by Glenn Miller and by the Andrews Sisters during World War II. The song speaks of two young lovers who promise to wait for each other while one of them is away serving in the war.

The song was originally titled "Anywhere the Bluebird Goes." And the melody was written by Sam H. Stept. His version was inspired by a nineteenth-century English folk song called "Long, Long Ago." The new version of the song, with lyrics by Lew Brown and Charles Tobias, debuted in the 1939 Broadway musical *Yokel Boy*. It wasn't until after the United States entered WWII in December 1941 that Brown and Tobias modified the lyrics to the version that is most known today, with the chorus ending with a line about marching home.

"Don't Sit Under the Apple Tree" sat at Your Hit Parade's first place from October 1942 through January 1943. No other war song held first place that long.

In May 1942, "Don't Sit Under the Apple Tree" was featured in the film *Private Buckaroo* with a performance by the Andrews Sisters. It featured a tap-dancing routine by the Jivin' Jacks and Jills. Soon after, the Andrews Sisters released the song with Decca

Records. Later in her life, Patty Andrews said that "Don't Sit Under the Apple Tree" was the most requested song of her career.

"Don't Sit Under the Apple Tree" is one of the few songs in American history to have three different popular versions on the radio and to be on Your Hit Parade at the same time.

In 2016, the Andrews Sisters' version was inducted into the Grammy Hall of Fame and remains one of the most iconic songs of the WWII era.

# FROM the HOME-FRONT KITCHEN

## US Navy's Soft Sugar Cookie Recipe from the Second World War

**Ingredients:**

2½ cups flour

1½ teaspoons baking powder

½ teaspoon salt

2 teaspoons nutmeg

½ cup and 1 tablespoon shortening

1 cup sugar

1 egg

¾ teaspoon vanilla

½ cup milk

**Directions:**

1. Preheat oven to 375 degrees.
2. Mix all ingredients at medium speed in large mixing bowl until smooth dough forms.
3. Drop dough by spoonful onto greased baking sheet.
4. Bake for 8 to 10 minutes. Remove cookies from pan while warm.

*Read on for a sneak peek of another exciting book*
*in the Whistle Stop Café Mysteries series!*

# AS TIME GOES BY

## BY RUTH LOGAN HERNE

irt flew into the air as Janet Shaw pulled her car up to the curb to drop off some much-needed baking supplies for the café's first commemorative "Lassies for Love" doughnut day.

Back in the 1940s, Salvation Army volunteers created delicious fried doughnuts drizzled with glaze or dusted with sugar to treat the troops going off to war. Their contributions of time and talent had put Dennison, Ohio, on the map during a rough time, and now she and her business partner and best friend, Debbie Albright, planned to celebrate that effort on specific holidays. Memorial Day. Labor Day. Veteran's Day. And the Fourth of July, which also happened to be her birthday.

In five days!

There was so much to do, but as she exited the car, she saw that their resident pooch had digging on his mind.

The fine loamy soil flew up, across, sideways, and even forward somehow, possibly defying laws of physics.

*Crosby…at it again.*

She spotted the soil-based storm just as Debbie dashed out the back door of the Whistle Stop Café. Some might call her friend's plunge into a whole new life as a café owner a midlife crisis.

Not Janet.

She preferred to think of their new partnership as an absolute blessing.

A blessing replete with a digging dog, flying dirt, and doughnuts.

"Hey, pup!" Debbie scolded. "We can't have miniature potholes tripping people every time they come this way. The insurance company is going to hike our rates due to hazardous conditions."

Crosby sat back, delighted with her attention and clearly proud of his efforts.

"Don't play innocent with me or even pretend you're following orders, because I know for a fact that you and Janet reached an agreement just a few days ago," she went on. "You, sir, are breaching that contract."

"Technically, he's not." Janet dusted her hands on her navy blue capris. They went well with her patriotic T-shirt, fitting for the coming holiday week. "Our agreement was of a more geographic variety," she explained. "He's close enough to the prescribed area to be on the right side of the border clause. Smart dog."

Debbie rolled her eyes. "It was more of the location, location, location-type contract, I presume?"

"Exactly." Janet opened the back door of her car, where the supplies sat. "I figured old habits die hard, and he and Harry are pretty set in their ways—"

"A ninety-five-year-old retired conductor and a seven-year-old dog."

Janet nodded. "Yes. So I gave Crosby explicit instructions to dig here. Not out front or on the side. I figured there's not much he can hurt over here under the tree. It's just enough off the beaten path."

"We got us some trouble, ladies?" Harry Franklin interrupted them. The elderly railroad man came their way from the side of the restored vintage depot. "My boy's a digger, sure enough, and I probably should have made him toe the line way back when, but nobody much cared about his digging before this place got so busy."

Janet reassured him quickly. "He's fine, Harry. I was just explaining to Debbie that Crosby and I renegotiated terms of use, and he's agreed to keep the majority of his digging on this side of the depot."

"A shady spot and a soft turn of earth, the stuff a dog's dreams are made of." Approval laced the old man's voice. "I sure am grateful you ladies don't mind a pair of old-timers hangin' around."

"Mind it?" Debbie crossed over and looped her arm through his. "Harry Franklin, you and Crosby are always welcome here."

Harry grinned at her. He'd lost some teeth along the way and he walked much slower these days, but Harry Franklin did all right for being a few years shy of a hundred. And he remembered more than most people forgot in a lifetime.

"Coffee, Harry?" asked Debbie. "And maybe some toast and eggs for our two favorite customers?"

Gracious as ever, Harry dipped his chin slightly. "We'd be most obliged, thank you."

He followed her inside.

Crosby started after them then paused. He gave the café a searching look. Almost longing.

But then he did a quick whirl-around and headed right back to the base of the tree. That oak had seemed old when Janet was a little girl. If it had survived all these years, a spot of digging here and there shouldn't disturb much. The thick roots were no longer completely buried. They pressed up, out of the earth, before stretching downward again.

She took a breath and gazed around, content. Content for the first time in a long time. She'd enjoyed working at the Third Street Bakery over in Uhrichsville for nearly twenty years. The Whipple family had been good to her and her family. And Charla Whipple had taught her so much. Janet had become the protégé, entrusted with many tricks of the trade, but the Whipples were retiring. The bakery was closing. So when Debbie had broached the idea of opening a café and bakery right here in the historic depot, Janet saw it as perfect timing. Her science-loving daughter would be leaving for her freshman year at Case Western Reserve University in Cleveland in less than two months. Tiffany was a delightful young woman and a wonderful student, and—

Her only child.

Knowing she was moving away had opened a hole in Janet's chest.

Focusing on this new venture with her best friend was a good way to suture that gap. Was it a coincidence to have it all fall into place like that? Or God's perfect timing? Janet sided with the latter, and she was grateful for it.

She turned to gather her purchases as dirt began flying again.

Then she paused when she heard a different sound.

The dog pummeled the soil like a champ, something he did at least twice a day, but this time was different. Sounded different.

Instead of the steady drum of Crosby's paws and the rain-down of rich topsoil against the tree, there was a new noise. Metallic and dull.

She edged in. "Crosby. Stop."

He looked puzzled and a trifle indignant, but she didn't blame him. She was messing with their agreed-upon contract. "What have you found, fella?"

He wagged his tail, now clearly pleased that she'd noticed his success.

She bent toward the hole. Something rusty and dirty lay beneath Crosby's excavating efforts. "What is this, boy?"

She reached in. Whatever it was wouldn't budge, and she couldn't pry it loose. On top of that, a good cook didn't work a busy public kitchen with dirt-stained hands. She stood up and crossed to the maintenance shed just up the tracks. There were a few tools in there, including gardening gloves and a small trowel for replacing the annual flowers they had put in pots and borders around the vintage building.

She donned the gloves and grabbed the trowel.

Crosby seemed unperturbed by her intrusion into his find. He sat back on his haunches and watched as she dug a narrow band around the item.

The dog crooned softly. Urging her on? Or just offering approval?

The trowel caught an edge. She gave it an extra thrust then pushed the handle down, using the small spade as a lever.

The hole wasn't deep, but deep enough that the dark, moist soil and thick shade made it hard to see inside.

The maneuver eventually worked, and the edge of the item lifted up. With a few more twists and turns, she was able to pull it out, tilting it to squeeze through the gaps made by the thick, branching roots.

It was a rectangular can of some sort, an old tin, like a metal cigar box. It slid up and out of the hole, dirty and rusted, a real mess.

She gave it a gentle shake. Nothing much moved, but it contained something. The weight indicated that.

Crosby leaned forward.

"It's your find, boy. I'm not claiming it," she assured him. "But I *am* going to wipe it down before I pry off the lid to see what's in it."

The dog seemed okay with that decision. When she stood, he reexamined the hole as if to make sure she'd done a good job. Content with her efforts, he yawned, moved aside, and did a three-circle spin before collapsing on a patch of soft green grass for his first morning nap.

She retrieved the bags from her back seat, carried everything inside, and, after putting the bags on the counter, moved to the service sink. Using wet paper towels, she washed down the top, bottom, and sides of the container, gradually revealing a vintage candy tin decorated with painted flowers. The name of the company started with an *S*, but that was about all she could make out.

"What's this? Buried treasure?" Debbie kept watch on the eggs while spreading soft butter—never margarine—on three pieces of white toast. Two for Harry. One for Crosby. The funny dog enjoyed his one-egg-on-toast morning meal on a regular basis.

"Buried, anyway. I'm not holding out hope for treasure," replied Janet as Harry leaned in to peek over the counter. "Crosby unearthed it. Well"—she made a face—"I helped. Let's dry it off…"

"And wedge it open?" suggested Debbie. "Away from your cooling cakes, of course."

"Far away," agreed Janet. She spread a dish towel on the counter and set the box on top. After applying a sturdy butter knife, she was able to loosen the lid.

Miniscule debris sprinkled onto the clean towel as the lid came loose. It wasn't an easy process. When one side inched up, the other pitched down, but then with one final nudge, the rusted old cover came free.

Harry reached over to lift it off.

A cluster of medals sat inside, nestled in a worn clutch of red velvet. The velvet was bunched around each one, creating individual pockets.

"That's why it didn't rattle when I shook it," Janet said. "I don't know what all these are, but I recognize that one right off." She pointed to the upper left corner.

"A Purple Heart." Harry's voice cracked. He stared at the medals. "I've seen more than a few of those in my time," he said. "Some for boys who came back. Some who didn't. But I've never seen a collection of medals like this."

"All one person?" Janet wondered aloud.

Harry frowned. "I don't know anyone who gathered brass like that."

"Stolen?" asked Debbie, but then she dismissed that idea. "If they were stolen, wouldn't the thief have returned for them at some time?"

"You'd think so. But maybe they couldn't," Janet said. "Maybe they got put in jail for something else and couldn't get back here and these medals have been hidden away for all these years. And if that's the case…" She straightened her shoulders and lifted her gaze. "There's only one thing we can do."

Debbie nodded understanding. She knew Janet's family history. "Find the rightful owners. But how?"

Harry shook his head. "I can't rightly say. I know there were plenty of medals given out during the war. A righteous number, well-deserved, but how do you find out who each one belongs to in a box of eleven? No, twelve," he corrected himself as he pointed out a much smaller lapel pin that had fallen into the corner between the velvet and the box. "It's not like they're marked or anything. How do we do this?"

Debbie drew a deep breath and exchanged a look with Janet. Janet's great-grandfather had served in World War II. Her grandfather and two great-uncles had served in Korea. Grandpa had been the only one to come home, and he'd spent a lifetime missing his two little brothers, so Janet knew exactly what they needed to do. She smiled at Debbie then faced the thoughtful man who'd grown old doing so much for so many. "Harry, my friend, we do whatever it takes."

**While you are waiting for the next fascinating story
in the *Whistle Stop Café Mysteries,* check out
some other Guideposts mystery series!**

# SAVANNAH SECRETS

Welcome to Savannah, Georgia, a picture-perfect Southern city
known for its manicured parks, moss-covered oaks, and antebellum
architecture. Walk down one of the cobblestone streets, and you'll
come upon Magnolia Investigations. It is here where two friends
have joined forces to unravel some of Savannah's deepest secrets.
Tag along as clues are exposed, red herrings discarded, and thrilling
surprises revealed. Find inspiration in the special bond between
Meredith Bellefontaine and Julia Foley. Cheer the friends on as they
listen to their hearts and rely on their faith to solve each new case
that comes their way.

*The Hidden Gate*
*The Fallen Petal*
*Double Trouble*
*Whispering Bells*
*Where Time Stood Still*
*The Weight of Years*
*Willful Transgressions*
*Season's Meetings*

*Southern Fried Secrets*
*The Greatest of These*
*Patterns of Deception*
*The Waving Girl*
*Beneath a Dragon Moon*
*Garden Variety Crimes*
*Meant for Good*
*A Bone to Pick*
*Honeybees & Legacies*
*True Grits*
*Sapphire Secret*
*Jingle Bell Heist*
*Buried Secrets*
*A Puzzle of Pearls*
*Facing the Facts*
*Resurrecting Trouble*
*Forever and a Day*

# MYSTERIES of MARTHA'S VINEYARD

Priscilla Latham Grant has inherited a lighthouse! So with not much more than a strong will and a sore heart, the recent widow says goodbye to her lifelong Kansas home and heads to the quaint and historic island of Martha's Vineyard, Massachusetts. There, she comes face-to-face with adventures, which include her trusty canine friend, Jake, three delightful cousins she didn't know she had, and Gerald O'Bannon, a handsome Coast Guard captain—plus head-scratching mysteries that crop up with surprising regularity.

*A Light in the Darkness*
*Like a Fish Out of Water*
*Adrift*
*Maiden of the Mist*
*Making Waves*
*Don't Rock the Boat*
*A Port in the Storm*
*Thicker Than Water*
*Swept Away*
*Bridge Over Troubled Waters*
*Smoke on the Water*
*Shifting Sands*
*Shark Bait*
*Seascape in Shadows*

*Storm Tide*
*Water Flows Uphill*
*Catch of the Day*
*Beyond the Sea*
*Wider Than an Ocean*
*Sheeps Passing in the Night*
*Sail Away Home*
*Waves of Doubt*
*Lifeline*
*Flotsam & Jetsam*
*Just Over the Horizon*

# MIRACLES & MYSTERIES of MERCY HOSPITAL

Four talented women from very different walks of life witness the miracles happening around them at Mercy Hospital and soon become fast friends. Join Joy Atkins, Evelyn Perry, Anne Mabry, and Shirley Bashore as, together, they solve the puzzling mysteries that arise at this Charleston, South Carolina, historic hospital—rumored to be under the protection of a guardian angel. Come along as our quartet of faithful friends solve mysteries, stumble upon a few of the hospital's hidden and forgotten passageways, and discover historical treasures along the way! This fast-paced series is filled with inspiration, adventure, mystery, delightful humor, and loads of Southern charm!

*Where Mercy Begins*
*Prescription for Mystery*
*Angels Watching Over Me*
*A Change of Art*
*Conscious Decisions*
*Surrounded by Mercy*
*Broken Bonds*
*Mercy's Healing*
*To Heal a Heart*
*A Cross to Bear*

*Merciful Secrecy*
*Sunken Hopes*
*Hair Today, Gone Tomorrow*
*Pain Relief*
*Redeemed by Mercy*
*A Genius Solution*
*A Hard Pill to Swallow*
*Ill at Ease*
*'Twas the Clue Before Christmas*

# A NOTE FROM the EDITORS

We hope you enjoyed this first exciting volume in the Whistle Stop Café Mysteries series, published by Guideposts. For over seventy-five years, Guideposts, a nonprofit organization, has been driven by a vision of a world filled with hope. We aspire to be the voice of a trusted friend, a friend who makes you feel more hopeful and connected.

By making a purchase from Guideposts, you join our community in touching millions of lives, inspiring them to believe that all things are possible through faith, hope, and prayer. Your continued support allows us to provide uplifting resources to those in need. Whether through our communities, websites, apps, or publications, we inspire our audiences, bring them together, and comfort, uplift, entertain, and guide them. Visit us at guideposts.org to learn more.

We would love to hear from you. Write us at Guideposts, P.O. Box 5815, Harlan, Iowa 51593 or call us at (800) 932-2145. Did you love *Under the Apple Tree*? Leave a review for this product on guideposts.org/shop. Your feedback helps others in our community find relevant products.

*Find inspiration, find faith, find Guideposts.*

## Shop our best sellers and favorites at
# guideposts.org/shop

# Find more inspiring stories in these best-loved Guideposts fiction series!

## Mysteries of Lancaster County

Follow the Classen sisters as they unravel clues and uncover hidden secrets in Mysteries of Lancaster County. As you get to know these women and their friends, you'll see how God brings each of them together for a fresh start in life.

## Secrets of Wayfarers Inn

Retired schoolteachers find themselves owners of an old warehouse-turned-inn that is filled with hidden passages, buried secrets, and stunning surprises that will set them on a course to puzzling mysteries from the Underground Railroad.

## Tearoom Mysteries Series

Mix one stately Victorian home, a charming lakeside town in Maine, and two adventurous cousins with a passion for tea and hospitality. Add a large scoop of intriguing mystery, and sprinkle generously with faith, family, and friends, and you have the recipe for *Tearoom Mysteries*.

## Ordinary Women of the Bible

Richly imagined stories—based on facts from the Bible—have all the plot twists and suspense of a great mystery, while bringing you fascinating insights on what it was like to be a woman living in the ancient world.

**To learn more about these books, visit Guideposts.org/Shop**